D0450192

A SCARY SCENE IN A SCARY MOVIE

Matt Blackstone

A Scary Scene in a Scary Movie

Farrar Straus Giroux
New York

Distributed in Canada by D&M Publishers, Inc.
Printed and bound in the United States of America
Designed by Andrew Arnold
First edition, 2011
1 3 5 7 9 10 8 6 4 2

macteenbooks.com

Library of Congress Cataloging-in-Publication Data

Blackstone, Matt.
A scary scene in a scary movie / Matt Blackstone. — 1st ed.
p. cm.
Summary: Rene, a high school freshman with obsessive-compulsive disorder, finds life to be like a scary movie, and even after he makes friends with the ultra-cool Giovanni he still feels responsible for saving his favorite teacher, dealing with his missing father, courting the beautiful Ariel, and trying to pretend to be normal for the school psychologist.
ISBN: 978-0-374-36421-2
[1. Obsessive-compulsive disorder—Fiction. 2. Emotional problems—Fiction. 3. Family problems—Fiction. 4. High schools—Fiction. 5. Schools—Fiction. 6. New York (N.Y.)—Fiction.] I. Title.

PZ7.B5332Sc 2011
[Fic]—dc22

2010021743

To my beautiful wife, Jamie

A Scary Scene in a Scary Movie

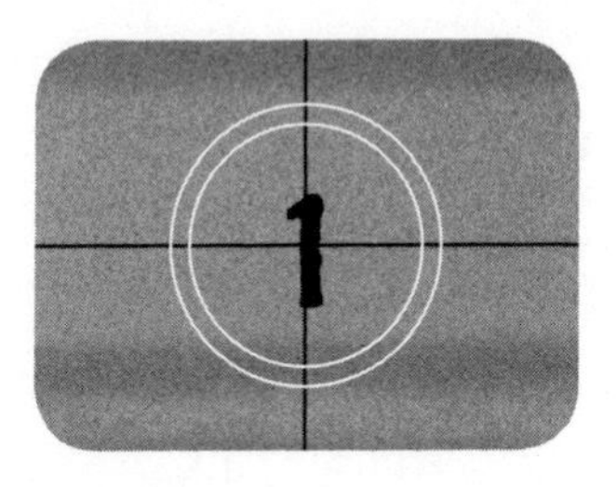

Legs are my favorite part. I never snap them off with a single bite. I nibble on them slowly as I work my way up. I crunch bony ankles, gnaw on slender calves. Knees are a delicacy; canine teeth are ideal for chipping cartilage. Thighs—oh sweet, sweet thighs—must be savored, eaten like a sacred drumstick. Thick and long and often hairy, a torso is best swallowed whole. The neck is delicious, but fragile: one bite and all I have left is a tiny head resting on my fingertips.

Animal crackers. They're a great snack, but they aren't great company. Real animals make better pets. Dogs *are* a man's best friend, but I am allergic to dogs. I am allergic to cats, guinea pigs, ferrets, gerbils, parrots, sheep, horses, and goats. So I chose bugs.

This summer, the last one before high school, I kidnapped fireflies on weekends and caterpillars on weekdays. I kept the fireflies in a jar until they went to sleep—permanently. I placed the caterpillars in the bathtub, where I tucked them in at night by covering their bodies with tissues.

Finding a bathtub full of caterpillars was a red flag for my mom.

"I've made an appointment for you to see the school psychologist," she said. "Several appointments."

If I don't like talking to people I know, why would I talk to strangers?

I have a Batman cape that I wear when I'm anxious. My mom says I shouldn't wear it to those meetings.

She thinks I'm nuts. She's had her suspicions ever since I was a kid, when I washed my hands until they were red and raw, talked to myself in public, ran away from anything numbered thirteen, smelled my hands more than forty times per day, ate my animal crackers in a specific order, and made creepy smiley faces out of napkins—even when I didn't want to.

I still do all those things—they are still part of my daily missions—because if I don't, I might die of AIDS, or someone close to me might die of a heart attack, or some stranger outside of my small town in Southern New Jersey might get blown up in a bus—and it'd be all my fault and I'd never live it down and I'd bury myself in my room for years and years and years until my Batman cape worked its magic or I became a superhero who didn't have to worry away death and cleanliness and guilt that never goes away, no matter how hard you scrub.

I don't tell my mom these things because I don't want to upset her. It's not like she has the time to deal with me anyway. She works two jobs: one as a hotel receptionist, the other as a part-time nurse. She doesn't get home till around 10:00 p.m. Sometimes, she doesn't come home at all.

“Follow my example and work hard, Rene,” she always tells me. That’s my name. Rene. It’s a boy’s name *and* a girl’s name, which is great if you’re getting a sex change. (I’m not.)

“Time is money,” my mom says. “Work hard for what you want.”

I know what I want. I’ve worked hard for it my entire life, but it still hasn’t happened. Not even for a day.

I want every*one* and every*thing* to leave me the hell alone.

THERE ARE MALLS IN MY TOWN, THREE OF THEM, WHERE kids who have friends like to shop, compare clothing labels, and talk about sports. And college. And college sports.

There are baseball diamonds in my town, five of them, where kids play catch for so long the only lights they see are fireflies, but they keep playing because they like being coordinated and popular and talking about driving permits and the new girl at school and the guidance counselor who says "education is the key to success" each and every time he opens his mouth, which is funny, but they agree with him, so it isn't really all that funny.

There are high schools in my town, two of them, where kids whose brains don't give them orders get excellent grades and do all their homework on time. I am not one of those kids, but I go to one of those high schools.

A couple weeks into school, the teachers *already* gave tons of homework.

"I was invisible when you handed that out," I tell my English teacher, Mr. Head.

I don't know why he doesn't believe me.

Sometimes I try to do homework, but, seriously, why should I read this stupid story about two old guys hunting in the woods? It's long, it's boring, and I'm tired. If time is money, I want my money back.

Not that I've ever had any money, except for my allowance, which comes only when my dad writes to me. So once every four years, I get paid. And only in $2 bills that arrive in an orange envelope. Leave it to Phil—that's what I've called him ever since he left my mom and me when I was eight—to pay me in outdated, overrated bills.

Along with the $2 bills, there's always a note that reads, "I'm not a monster." It's an inside joke. The first time Phil took me to the zoo, I was scared of the animals, especially the apes. When I saw the hairy orangutan rattling its cage, I jumped up and down, yelling, "Look, Daddy, it's a monster!"

I love inside jokes because I like jokes and because it's more comfortable being on the inside than it is on the outside. The $2 bills are also an inside joke because six years ago, the year he left us, my dad drove my mom and me to Monticello, which is a fancy name for Thomas Jefferson's old white house. On our way out, Phil slipped a security guard a $50 bill in exchange for twenty-five $2 bills.

"That's what I call highway robbery," he told me. "'Cause in thirty years, when these babies collect interest, he'll be kicking himself in the wiener. You hang on to these bills, you hear?"

Phil has a way with words because he is a writer, a good writer, but has never been published. I want to be a writer, too, because I want to be better than him. I *need* to be a better, more successful writer than Phil.

Until then, I keep Phil's $2 bills in a frame above my bed. My mom says it's healthy to keep souvenirs of Phil and show them to my friends.

The problem is that I don't have many friends. The ones I *do* have, my mom dismisses as either invisible or inappropriate. I thought we had finally agreed on one, though: Mr. Head, my English teacher.

If you're wondering how I know that Mr. Head and I are friends, it's because every morning Mr. Head says to my class, "Good morning, my friends."

"Teachers don't count, Rene," my mom informed me one night as she tucked me into bed. That's right, she still tucks me in. I mean, it's not like I need a night-light or anything juvenile like that, just a tuck. Especially since school started.

I'm a freshman. I use hair spray, hair gel, and hair mousse. And Old Spice deodorant, fresh scent. I can quote from all the Batman movies. I am very organized and very clean. I use soap instead of hand sanitizer because I heard that hand sanitizer gets you high and kills brain cells. Because I need to hang on to all the brain cells I have left, I use soap. Lots of it.

I like things *my way*. For example, even though we're only a month into school, my routine is as permanent as permanent marker: I like to eat cereal—Lucky Charms for good luck—before the bus picks me up for school, where I bubble in the magical code of abacadaba *so* perfectly within the lines on Scantron tests that I never finish, worry about my safety instead of taking notes, wash my hands four times before I eat my sandwich of chunky peanut butter and strawberry jelly on wheat bread alone in a packed, screaming lunchroom until next period, when I refuse to change and therefore fail gym and sit in the bleachers until the bell grants me permission to walk home seven-eighths of a mile to my house, where I savor my second bowl of Lucky Charms while watching cartoons and convincing myself that I'll do my vocabulary homework after I complete my mission to comb the streets for good luck coins and perfect rubber bands to fix around my wrist until it gets dark or I get hungry enough to wash my hands four times and eat a microwavable meal while beating myself in chess and checking the window for Mom's headlights, so I can tell her how well I'm doing in school so that she'll tuck me in and I can fall asleep as I plan which cereal I'll eat in the morning.

If I do any one of these things wrong or even slightly out of order, I might break my neck or my arm or hopefully just my ankle; Phil might reappear; a terrorist might blow up my house; Mr. Head might quit; and/or I might never ever make a single friend, which would be doomsday because there's this one freakishly tall classmate named Giovanni who I would like to make my friend. I nicknamed him "Giovanni the Giant" until I learned his last name is Caperna, which obviously sounds like a superhero name, the Caped Crusader, and even though I'm the only one who wears a cape, not him, I nicknamed him "Giovanni the Caped Crusader." I really admire Giovanni the Caped Crusader because he, unlike me, is a social butterfly. Since most people like being social and everybody likes butterflies, I think I'm the only person at school that Giovanni hasn't talked to—and he's only been at my school for four days! He's a transfer student, which means he should feel lonely and isolated in a new school, but even the principal, who doesn't like *anybody,* likes Giovanni. One time in the hallway, he said to Giovanni, "Nice hair, young man. I used to have hair like that, but that was many moons ago." Then he sighed. I sighed, too.

Giovanni's puffy, curly hair adds two more inches to his height. Everything about Giovanni is cool. He's not jock-cool or rocker-cool; more like wise, old man–cool, even though, like me, he's fourteen. I know that because on the first day of school, he wore a T-shirt that read, "Being fourteen rocks."

I'm no expert or anything—I've only been fourteen for the last thirty-seven days—but I think Giovanni might be wrong.

Take this stupid homework assignment, the one I've been reading for the last two hours, about two old guys hunting in the woods.

Two old guys hunting in the woods. Need I say more?

THE ANSWER TO THAT QUESTION IS "NO." I LEARNED THAT when Mr. Head, my tall, big-boned English teacher, got mad, I mean firecracker mad, at me during yesterday's class. It wasn't even that big of a deal, but leave it to Mr. Head to make a mountain out of an anthill. Or an anthill out of a mole. You know what I'm trying to say. Anyway, I was trying to listen to him because we're friends, and plus he's an English teacher and I hoped he could help me become a better writer—maybe teach me how to put my thoughts down on paper—but he was droning on about how he wants to teach us *Romeo and Juliet* but doesn't trust us enough. I wouldn't trust us if I were him either. My classmates, other than me of course, don't pay attention to him. I mean, they weren't even *looking* at Mr. Head while he shouted, "Enough! Listen up! Hold up! Eyes up here! Eyes on speaker! Hand up if you hear me! Trees up! Nerds up!" He kept picking new expressions to see if we'd magically respond.

We didn't. So he got louder. "Yo, everybody! Let me see your ready position! Close your mouths! Be quiet! I'll wait! That's right: I'll *wait* for you to be quiet! I'll wait all day and all night—well, not *all* night because I *do* have a life, but I'll definitely wait all *day*. I'll wait all day long. I'll wait till the cows come home . . ."

Some kid in the back row mooed. At least he was listening.

Mr. Head sat down at the front of the room. He breathed hard, stared at his shoelaces, picked his nails, clenched and unclenched his fists.

Since I didn't have anyone to talk to, I walked over to him, making sure not to step on any of the lines on the floor so that something scary wouldn't happen to me or my mom or anyone that might become my friend. I don't know what got into me. I guess I was so bored that I tuned out the voice inside my head that shouts *DON'T DO ANYTHING STUPID*! whenever I'm around other humans.

I moved to the side of Mr. Head. He was a dead animal,

limp and defeated. I smelled my left hand, because that's what I do when I'm nervous, which is about six to eight hours per day, depending on whether it's a weekend or weekday. Since it was a weekday, I'd already smelled my left hand thirty-two times. (The smell of my own skin reminds me that I'm a perfectly normal human being. But you can never be too sure. Of anything.)

I put my hand on Mr. Head's large, sweaty shoulder, and in my most sympathetic tone—the one my mom uses when she talks about Phil—I said, "I feel bad, Mr. Head. I don't want you to waste your time or anything."

"Look at this," he said, smacking his hands on his lap. "At my life. At this room. At this class. Need I say more, Rene?"

"Yes," I said. Recalling my mom's advice about Phil, I told Mr. Head, "Expressing your feelings can be therapeutic."

That's when Mr. Head hung his head and let out a low, guttural moan—the sound Phil used to make after coming home from work. He said it's "the sound of a man staring down a dead-end career all the way to the grave." Mr. Head, the second dying man I'd met, rose from his chair.

He pivoted like a slow ballerina until he had his back to the class.

Then he banged his head against the chalkboard. The heavy thud silenced the class as Mr. Head kept right on banging his forehead. Again. And again. And again.

THAT AFTERNOON, MR. HEAD HAD HALL DUTY. DESPITE the white chalk and the growing red welt on his forehead, he sat ramrod straight in his chair, his chin up. I could tell he was trying not to cry because I've seen that look on my mom's face every time she talks about Phil. I didn't want to be the guy to push Mr. Head over the edge.

Giovanni wasn't as prudent. He walked over to Mr. Head and said, "Hey, brother man, I heard what happened. But it's not your fault. So don't even worry about it."

"I—thank you, Gio," Mr. Head said, as if he and Giovanni were best pals.

"Don't sweat it, brother man," Giovanni said. "Kids these days can be pretty nasty. Hey, you're not pondering a career change, are you?"

"I—"

"Don't do anything drastic, Mr. Head. God knows I've been down that bumpy road of self-doubt before. Tell you what, sleep on it for a few days and then play it by ear."

"I wasn't going to—"

"You know what, Mr. Head," Gio said, bending down. "You're good money, Mr. Head. You're b'noodles. You're something special. You remember that."

A pride bordering on admiration welled up on Mr. Head's wide face.

Giovanni must have sensed it, too, because he nudged him in the arm. "Hey, bottom line, nobody's perfect," Giovanni said, pointing at a large jagged chip on his front tooth. "But when you got a gift like you do, you gotta believe in yourself. And if someone gets in your way, you say, 'Get off my biscuit' and get on with your life."

Mr. Head's lower lip quivered as he stood up to shake Giovanni's hand. Even standing, Mr. Head was at least six inches shorter than Giovanni.

"You have no idea how much that means to me, Gio," said Mr. Head. "You truly do have insight, sir, you truly do."

Giovanni shrugged. "I only speak the truth."

Hearing the bell, Giovanni elbowed Mr. Head in the arm and said, "Give 'em hell, you hear?"

Mr. Head raised his arms to hug Giovanni, but Giovanni had already blended into a sea of students lugging their textbooks to fourth period class.

Phil once said he'll always remember the first time he heard Bob Dylan's music: "Mind-blowing. An automatic epiphany. Inspirational." Before today, I hated the word "inspirational," and I certainly didn't believe in epiphanies, let alone automatic ones. Even *I* know nothing is automatic, except for superheroes, and that inspiration is as real as the tooth fairy. Besides, Bob Dylan? Come on, Bob Dylan's not even his real name. It's Robert Zimmerman. How inspirational is *that*?

But last night, after my mom tucked me in and told me it wasn't my fault that Mr. Head exploded in class or that Phil left her when I was still young, I put on my Batman cape, got down on my knees, and prayed that I would someday be friends with Giovanni.

Or at least walk near him.

Now that Giovanni is in my life, everything is changing. Well, not everything. I still smell my hands and eat alone and sit in the bleachers during gym class. But now I'm *looking around* while I walk, instead of at the ground. For instance, during lunch today, I looked for Giovanni in the lunchroom. He wasn't there. So everything didn't change. I wanted it to, but it didn't.

So at the end of the day, I walked home by myself and savored my second bowl of cereal—Lucky Charms for good luck—while watching cartoons and convincing myself that I'll do my vocabulary homework after I comb the streets for good luck coins and the perfect rubber band to fix around my wrist until it gets dark or I get hungry enough to wash my hands four times and eat a microwavable meal while beating myself in chess and checking the window for mom's headlights, so I can tell her how well I'm doing in school so that she'll tuck me in and I can fall asleep as I plan which cereal I'll eat in the morning.

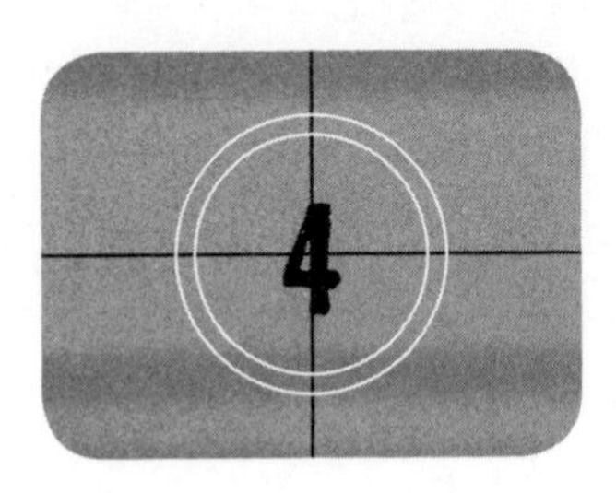

MY EYES ARE FOCUSED ON MY DIGITAL BATMAN WATCH because the moment is almost here. No, it's more than a moment; it's a remembrance, a dedication, an anniversary of what happened in this exact spot at this exact time.

Batman never lies. The moment has arrived. It's been exactly one week; 604,800 seconds have passed since Giovanni temporarily saved Mr. Head during his hall duty. I'm waiting for Giovanni outside the lunchroom once again, but I can't wait forever because it's been 192 minutes since my last meal, a bowl of Lucky Charms, so I walk inside and take a seat.

Besides cereal, my favorite food is a Frosty, which they only serve at comfortable, yet classy restaurants like Wendy's. I can't buy one now, though. You can't get a Frosty in the school lunchroom because it isn't a comfortable or classy place, so while not drinking a Frosty, I hear people talking about Mr. Head. I am not included in these conversations because, like I said, I eat alone; but even when I'm not eating alone—which is rare but it does happen on holidays—I have this creepy habit: I grab a napkin and tear at its edges until I have three small pieces and one big piece; the three small pieces I roll into tiny balls and the one larger piece I curve into a horseshoe. Then I align my smiley face.

At this very instant, my smiley face isn't really smiling because Mr. Head is a popular topic of conversation for each of the kids sitting at tables to my right. They say that Mr. Head is "dark," "shady," "shocking," "weak," "a waste of, like, time and space," "obviously schizophrenic," "an uncoordinated fathead," "Richard Head," "a dickhead," "the opposite of Che Guevara," and "frighteningly altruistic."

Different tables say different things because kids sit by groups. I tell my mom that I'm *in between* each of the groups, that I share some similarities with each of them and that I'm trying to decide where I best fit in.

But I don't fit with the Devilblackcoats, who look like a cross between Harry Potter's friends and Bella's vampire crew. I mean, I'm similar to the Devilblackcoats because I have pale skin, hate my father, and love Harry Potter books, but the similarities end there. For one, their devil rings are too powerful: I've heard they can transport someone straight to hell. Plus, Devilblackcoats always look like they're at a funeral; they don't even smile at happy things like the school bell ringing at the end of the day.

And I don't fit with the Bigbulletholes—you know, the ones with such big holes in their ears that it looks like someone shot them with big bullets; who slice up their blue jeans until white thread hangs like spaghetti over their knees and ankles; who spike their hair and wear black T-shirts with the word "straightedge" (which means they aren't gay) written in black marker on masking tape, or red T-shirts with a picture of a long-haired guy with a curly mustache and the words "Che Guevara" underneath it. I, too, am straightedge, but I hate bullets and loud music and I don't know or even *want* to know who Che Guevara is, so I don't hang with them.

I definitely don't fit with the Smartypants who wear polo shirts, read *The New Yorker*, carry an organizer to plan their days, and say "of course" and "obviously" after everything you say. Just the other day, I walked into English class looking tired. A Smartypants said, "You look sleepy." "I didn't have a good snooze last night," I answered, so he said, "Obviously, you mean 'slumber.' A 'snooze' connotates a nap or one dozing off, whereas 'slumber' suggests a night's sleep. Of course, that's what you should have said."

If you try to start a conversation with a Smartypants by saying, "These french fries are good," they roll their eyes and tell you why the french fries you're eating are actually, factually, gross. If you disagree with them, they debate you, listing the merits of a perfect french fry until they declare themselves the undefeated, undisputed champion of common knowledge. If you still disagree, they shove french fries up your nose until you admit that you're wrong and they're right, forever and ever, amen. And even if you don't want to talk to a Smartypants, they talk to you. They're the ones who in elementary school tell you that your epidermis is showing, or force you to spell "I CUP," or tell you to raise your arms in the air and say the word "geometry" very, very slowly. And when you don't get the joke, they say, "You *really* don't get it? Yo, he *really, really* doesn't get it!" until your face is the color of blood. Then they laugh at you, not with you.

There's really only one group that *doesn't* laugh at you: the Angels. They're the only group not talking about Mr. Head right now. The Angels are the girls who get all As and Bs because they actually study; the ones who look good in anything they wear and don't even know it because they never talk about it or flaunt the label; the ones who'd pick something off the floor if you dropped it and say "You're welcome" after you thanked them; the ones who throw their trays out in the lunchroom; the ones who read books and then lend them out without saying "Now don't lose it or anything"; the ones who make a wish when a ladybug lands on their shirt; the ones who could make me fly for a whole year by waving to me in the hallway or saying hello to me, even if they didn't mean to.

The Angels don't know they're Angels, but even if they *did* know it, they wouldn't say it; and even if they *said* it, which they probably wouldn't, they would never use the word "like" while saying it. Like the Likegirls who, like, say "like" after every, like, sentence, and drive me, like, bananas, because, like, I want to talk with them and, like, kiss them or at least smell their hair, but I, like, hate when they, like, make me feel like an ugly caterpillar who is so ugly that, like, he needs a tissue put over his, like, body *and* face before he, like, goes to sleep and dreams of, like, cereal.

The Likegirls like the Cutters, who cut most of their

classes but always go to gym and lunch, which is the dumbest thing I've ever heard. If I were okay with breaking rules and doing illegal things like cutting class, I would cut gym and lunch forever. But the Cutters *love* lunch, which is terrible for Mr. Head because they don't have very nice things to say about him, even though they barely go to his class.

My mom wants me to join at least one of the groups in school. She says that a young man as smart as me is bound to find a group of smart friends. My mom is not a liar, but I don't think she's telling the truth about me being smart. I mean, my grades are hideously ugly, and I don't understand why nobody likes Mr. Head. Though he hasn't yet made me a better writer, Mr. Head *is* my friend, even if my mom disapproves. If you're wondering why my mom disapproves of Mr. Head, it's because she doesn't want me to get hurt. That's what she says about everyone. That's what she'd say about Giovanni.

But I *have* to be friends with Giovanni. I *have* to.

If you're wondering if I'm gay, the answer is no. In the interest of full disclosure (I love that phrase because it reminds me of television), I've had a crush on girls since I was five. I think they're pretty. They smell a whole lot better than me. I picture them naked 5 to 9 percent of my day, depending on whether it's a weekend or a weekday. I desperately want to kiss a live, human girl/lady/woman on the lips, especially a freshman named Ariel Merriweather, who looks good in any type of weather. She is an Angel. The Angel of Angels. One time, I was standing next to her while she sneezed. I said,

"God bless you," and offered her a tissue. As she took it, she touched my hand. I didn't want to wash my hands that day or even the next month, but if I didn't wash them, something awful could've happened to me or my family, and I'd never see or smell Ariel again. My Ariel has red hair, just like Ariel from *The Little Mermaid.* When my Ariel is around, my left hand smells like red roses. When Ariel walks by, I breathe in deeply and quickly, because her scent lingers for 4.8 seconds. I've timed it on my Batman watch. If I could bottle up the smell of Ariel walking by, I would be a millionaire. Ariel, though, is the type of girl who wouldn't like me any more if I had that kind of money. She's naturally an Angel—that's what I love about her.

But I never want to actually *be* a girl or switch places with a girl, not even an especially beautiful one like Ariel Merriweather. I do, however, want to switch places with Giovanni.

I want to be him. Of that I am certain.

I AM ALSO CERTAIN THAT I *DON'T* WANT TO BE JOHNNY VAN Slyke. He is the opposite of a superhero. He is an evildoer.

When I got braces in the sixth grade, Johnny Van Slyke said I'd never be able to board an airplane because I'd set off the metal detector and hold up everyone on the plane while the Feds cuffed me and grilled me in a sweaty room, blowing cigarette smoke in my face until I passed out.

Remember how I told you that I use hair spray and deodorant? I started using both in the seventh grade. When Johnny Van Slyke found out that I used deodorant, he pulled me aside and, with a serious teacher face, told me that deodorant causes Alzheimer's disease. When I got home that day, I asked my mom about Alzheimer's and she said it's what Grandpa used to have before he died. Although I sometimes want to forget that my name is Rene, I don't want to forget everything else, so I stopped using deodorant for fourteen months until one of my teachers called my mom and told her that I smelled.

Oh, hair spray—Johnny Van Slyke told me that the chemicals in hair spray and shampoo cause baldness. Since I didn't want to be anything like Phil, I stopped using hair spray—and washing my hair—until another teacher told my mom that I smelled.

And now, one week A.G. (After Gio) helped Mr. Head, on my way out of lunch, Johnny Van Slyke elbows me in the ribs and bites me on the shoulder. Hard.

"Why are you biting me?" I ask.

His teeth still in my shoulder, he mumbles, "Because I didn't have time to eat lunch."

An hour later, I'm waiting for Ms. Adelman, the school psychologist, even though I *should* be on a gurney being rushed to the emergency room to be checked for rabies from Johnny Van Slyke's bite. I know you get rabies mostly from dogs but it really wouldn't hurt to be checked for this or any other infectious disease, and I want to tell someone about this emergency, maybe Ms. Adelman—if she lets me in on time.

We have an appointment at 2:00 sharp. My Batman watch is never wrong, so I am certain that it's exactly 2:00. Unless she opens the door in three seconds, she will be late, as usual, which will make me not want to speak to her, as usual.

She's late.

The waiting room looks like a scary scene in a scary movie. White paint is peeling off the walls. When I touch the ground with my left index finger, dust stays on my finger. I want to wash my hands but I have to wait until after the appointment because I need to convince Ms. Adelman that I am cured.

Her office is making this difficult. There are invisible cobwebs with invisible spiders climbing up an empty magazine rack—and it smells like old people.

Ms. Adelman finally opens the door. She's three minutes late, so obviously I don't want to talk to her. She invites me in anyway.

Two leather chairs, the stale smell of manila folders and yellow notebooks, a clean beige carpet that isn't clean enough, framed plaques—Bachelor of Arts, Rutgers University; Master of Psychology, Seton Hall University—with Susan Adelman's name inscribed on them.

I grab a seat and tell her my day is going fine.

"Are you sure it's going fine?" she asks, looking up at me over her glasses.

"Yes."

"Still thinking about Phil?"

"No."

"Did something happen?"

"No."

"Did someone frighten you?"

"No."

"Did Johnny Van Slyke frighten you again?"

"No."

"Rene . . ." She clears her throat. "Anxiety, obsessive thoughts, compulsive behavior—these are serious things. Common—actually, *quite* common—but serious."

"Nothing is wrong with me. I'm cured."

She bites her lower lip. "You know, Rene, we talked about anxiety quite a bit last session . . . Do you remember what we spoke about?"

"No."

"We spoke about how your maturity level may be behind that of your classmates. Remember how we talked about ways to overcome that?"

"No."

"We can be a good team, Rene, but we need to work together. Do you want to be a good team?"

I shrug my shoulders.

"Okay . . . Rene, do you remember how we talked about facing your fears?"

"No."

"Do you remember how I taught you to take three deep breaths when you're nervous . . . and *then* think?"

"No."

"Like this," she says, taking three breaths.

As if I don't know how to breathe . . .

She points at my hands. "Why do you think you make smiley faces?" In my lap, a smiley face made out of tissue stares back at me. I stuff the eyes, nose, and mouth into my pockets.

"It's nothing," I mutter.

Ms. Adelman stares at me for a long time without speaking, which means she has something important to say.

"Are you happy, Rene?" she asks.

"No," I say. Then I stare at *her* for a long time without speaking. When she is about to open her mouth, I tell her, "No, I'm not happy, but I will be when I leave."

"Then you may go."

I don't look back. I whisper goodbye to her dirty waiting room with its old-people smell and invisible spiders and walk into the hallway.

Maybe because I had Lucky Charms for breakfast or maybe because I have five rubber bands on my left wrist and six on my right, or maybe it's because I actually did my vocabulary homework last night, but it's suddenly becoming a great day. No, it is becoming such a sterling, magnanimous day that we're getting out of school early!

One student just shouted down the hall that it's been raining so hard and for so long that the principal will be dismissing students an hour early.

I don't have an umbrella but I have a hood, because I wear hooded sweatshirts to school every day. People are always telling me to stop wearing "hoodies *every single day*," to which I respond, "I've never even *worn* a 'hoodie'; I only wear hooded sweatshirts."

Anyway, not wanting to postpone my afternoon bowl of cereal, I put on my hood, wave goodbye to classmates who don't wave back, and leap into the rain like Batman . . .

The rain is blinding but I don't need to see because I'm in the army and I can run like a sprinter and leap like a long jumper and fly like Batman. Roger that. I'm flying like Batman through the torrential rain soaking my clothes and hair and books. My shirt is already a wet sponge but it doesn't matter because I'm running and flying so fast the air will dry me like a supersonic hand dryer. It's a dangerous war, snipers everywhere, but I'll make it out alive because I'm bulletproof and fast; faster than anyone; faster than the cars in the parking lot; faster than a speeding bullet because my arms are wings and I'm tilting from side to side because it's good to be talented and breathing and beautiful and wet on my knees—on my knees? Roger that. My ankle! My ankle, my shirt, my hair, my backpack—floating with me in this brown puddle getting bigger from screeching tires and laughter. "It's not funny," I hear myself spit; "over and out," I mumble because I need to run away but it hurts to stand so I think I'll lie down for a few minutes, but I know I'll never wake up because it's not a dream, roger that, and all I want is to be over and out of this place, this puddle. My arms are being lifted and I'm wobbling and confused and looking up and wiping the rain from my face with my soaked shirt and I can feel someone standing me up and asking me if I'm okay, and I'm wiping wet stuff from my eyes, but I don't know if it's rain or tears because Giovanni, my Caped Crusader, my Batman, is towering over me.

"Can you walk on it?" he asks. His voice is deeper than I remember.

I look down at the puddle I'm still standing in. "I can't walk on water," I say.

"No, your ankle, can you walk on it?"

"Yeah, I think I can. Thank you."

He reaches out his hand. "Giovanni. The name's Giovanni."

"I know."

"How?" he asks.

"How am I walking?"

"No, how did you know my name?"

"From, um, Mr. Head."

"Richy?"

"No, Mr. Head. I heard your name from Mr. Head."

"Same dude. Richy, you know, short for Richard."

"That's *really* his name, *Richard Head*?"

"It is, but it's only a name after all, like Rene is a name."

"Rene is *my* name."

He smiles. "You don't make things very easy, do you?"

"How, how, did you know—?"

"Your name? Everyone knows you, come on."

"Knows *me*?"

"Are you cold, brother man? Your teeth are chattering."

To get them to stop, I bite down. Hard. My tongue is bleeding. I can taste it.

An SUV accelerates through a puddle, drenching my hooded sweatshirt with dirty rainwater. Another car whooshes by, splashing mud in my face.

"You got an umbrella?" Giovanni asks.

I tell my face to answer. It doesn't.

"The buses already left," he says, "so we gotta walk. I live by the post office. About a half a mile up the road."

"You want to walk *with me*?"

"Unless you don't want me to . . ."

Giovanni is holding one of those really large and fancy double-person umbrellas. Despite its size, the umbrella isn't really working: the rain either attacks me from the side or from the sidewalk. Every few steps, I wipe my face.

"Some storm, huh?" Giovanni says, squinting. "Do you like the rain?"

I want to answer him but I'm too focused on the cracks in the sidewalk. If I step on them, any of them, Gio will run away and I'll never make another friend ever again, especially one as cool as Giovanni.

On our right, construction workers sit under the awning of a half-finished row of stores. Brewed Awakenings and Martin's Magic and Joe's Pizza are being replaced by Starbucks and Staples and Papa John's.

"Don't like stepping on the cracks?" Gio asks.

"Yeah, I mean no, I mean . . ."

Silence. I've scared him off. Why couldn't I be cool? Relaxed and smooth like Will Smith in every summer movie. *DO SOMETHING. SAY SOMETHING. THIS IS WHAT YOU PRAYED FOR. GOD IS REAL. NOW SAY SOMETHING. Ready, one, two, three, SAY SOMETHING. Ten, nine, eight, seven, six, five, four, three, two, one, NOW. NOW!*

"You're tall," I blurt out. "And your puffy hair makes you look even taller."

"You're not," he says. "And your buzz cut makes you look even shorter."

What now? Ten, nine, eight . . . I look away from him, across the street, at Clearview, a new housing development with a gated entrance. As a car pulls up to the gate, a mustachioed man with a button-down "Clearview" shirt rises from his chair and glares into the car window. It looks like he wants to fight. If the guard were a superhero, I'd name him Beagle Eyes. The driver waves. Beagle Eyes, looking disappointed, opens the gate.

"I'm six feet tall," Giovanni says. "How tall are you?"

"I'm sixty-one inches."

He laughs. Wait, at me or at the joke? I used to play ping-pong in my head with this question all the time: He was laughing at me. *No, he wasn't, it was just a joke.* It wasn't funny. *No, it wasn't, but he wasn't laughing at you.* Then why did he say it like that? *I don't know. Maybe he was laughing at you.*

That would go on for days. My mom taught me that, when unsure about a joke, it's best to swallow some pride and ask. Since my mom's always right, I ask Gio if he's laughing at me or the joke.

"At the fact that you're not joking," he says.

"Oh."

"It's cool, Rene," Giovanni says. "Talking with you is b'noodles."

"Ba—"

"Noodles."

"Wait, *what* kind of noodles?"

"*B'*noodles. Pronounced BUH-noodles. It's an expression that means 'uniquely cool.' I made it up because b'noodles is uniquely cool and fun to say. Get it?"

I get it: Giovanni and I are best friends. Instead of telling him that, I talk about small things. "This is a nice umbrella."

He chuckles. "I stole it."

"You *stole* it?"

"Don't get preachy on me, brother man," Giovanni says. "I'm *proud* of stealing umbrellas . . . I teach them a lesson."

"Who?"

"Anyone with an umbrella. It's a grand scheme that I invented myself."

"Like you invented b'noodles," I say to prove I am following.

"Right . . . Anyway, what I do is simple. Here, hold the umbrella. Actually, you know what, instead of telling you, I'll show you. That's what Richy—I mean, Mr. Head—is always telling us to do about our writing anyway. You know, Mr. Head's golden rule."

"Show, don't tell."

"Exactly, now watch," he says, handing me the umbrella.

Giovanni hops over five puddles to reach a freshman who shares the same lunch period as me. His name's Bryan O'Toole. He has red hair and a jelly belly. Sometimes, during lunch, I laugh because I tell myself that if he has hair on his stomach like Phil does, he could say, "I have a strawberry jelly belly."

Giovanni approaches Bryan and his maybe hairy stomach, and ducks under his umbrella.

"Mind if you share?" Giovanni asks.

"Get the hell out of my umbrella, you goddamn crazy son of—"

Before Bryan finishes his sentence, Giovanni snatches the umbrella out of his hand and scurries away.

Bryan remains a statue for 3.6 seconds, and then shouts, "Hey, loony tune, what gives?"

In a composed, yet biting tone that only teachers use, Giovanni hollers, "Didn't your mama ever teach you that sharing is caring?"

Giovanni hands me Bryan's umbrella and points me forward. "Don't worry, brother man, like the rest of them, he's too stunned to do anything."

I smile that proud smile that Mr. Head had shown Giovanni after his pep talk. It occurs to me that Mr. Head was correct when he told Gio: "You truly do have insight, sir, you truly do."

Sensing one of those movie moments of understanding and friendship between us, I think about asking if it'd be all right if I call him "Gio," like Mr. Head had done during their heroic conversation.

"You're welcome," Giovanni says.

"Huh?"

"For your umbrella."

"Oh, thanks. But, well, why do you steal?"

He smirks. "Because I can. Because . . . why not?"

"But I thought stealing was—"

"Look, I'm not a kleptomaniac or anything crazy like that. I simply take what I think should rightfully be mine."

"But everyone will think—"

"Ah, I see you're still imprisoned. If you ever liberate yourself from your shackles, you'll realize that the general public is always wrong. And even if it's right—not that it ever happens—so what? We're all individuals, so we should act like individuals. I, as an individual, like taking umbrellas."

"But why?"

Up ahead, on the Little League baseball diamond, rain falls so heavily that the dirt infield bubbles like a boiling pot of coffee. This makes me happy. Giovanni's stealing does not.

"Look, brother man," he says. "I answer to a higher calling. It's my moral duty to give, or 'giveth,' if you will. In this case, I giveth manners. I also, in case you didn't notice, giveth and taketh away shelter from the storm. But I'm no superhero or anything."

"Yes you are, you're my Batman," I say instead of think. I smack my mouth with my left hand and slump my head toward the puddles.

"Easy there, brother man," he says. "Like I was saying, I'm no Batman or Superman or anything, but I'm proud of my umbrella shtick."

"Stick?"

"Shtick. It's Yiddish, for, um, routine, or um, performance. Get it?"

I don't. I am too focused on giving him a superhero name.

"The Umbrella Avenger," I suggest. "For your umbrella stick."

He punches me in the shoulder, like pals do to each other.

"The Umbrella Avenger, that's b'noodles," he says. "How about Rainman?"

I give him a thumbs-up because most good superhero names end in "man."

"Or the Umbrella Fella?" he offers.

I give him a thumbs-down because it rhymes. Too childish.

"The Caped Crusader," I suggest. "I like that one the best. I named you that a few weeks ago."

He chuckles. "You *named* me that?"

"As a nickname. Because your last name is Caperna."

It takes him a few seconds to understand, but once he does, he punches me again, like a pal.

"Well, this is my house," he says, pointing to a one-story dark-green house with brown shutters. It's a lot smaller than the other houses on the block—it's even smaller than *my* house—but it looks like nature, which is a thing I love.

"See you tomorrow," he says. As he walks toward the front door, I don't move or breathe because I sense another movie moment coming.

I guess he does, too, because as he gets to his front stoop, he turns around and says, "And, Rene, you can call me Gio."

Having a friend, another thing I love.

Superheroes acquire their powers from different sources. Spider-Man was bitten on the neck by a radioactive spider; Superman lived on the planet Krypton; I became friends with Gio. That's how I got my powers.

Only four hours after Giovanni said I could call him Gio, I feel like I can do anything! Well, almost anything—I can't spin webs like Spider-Man, but I have his courage and maybe even his superhuman vision. Gio gave it to me.

If Phil were here—thank God he's not—but if he were, I would tell him off. I'd give him a bloody nose and not offer him a tissue to wipe it up. If Johnny Van Slyke messed with me, I'd bite him on the shoulder and tell him, "I already ate lunch; I just wanted to bite your shoulder. If you don't leave me alone, I'll bite the whole thing off."

And I wouldn't need to wash my hands *or* mouth. Not tonight.

Tonight I look my demons in the eye and say, "You don't even look like demons. You look like the bugs in my bathtub." Tonight I will march to the front entrance of Radcliffe High School and conquer my fears of the gym, the hallways, the lunchroom, even the classrooms. Tonight I am no longer afraid of them, as I am no longer afraid of myself.

At least for tonight. Before my powers run out, I need to hurry. I need to leave. Right now. At night. Getting tucked in by my mom after picking up rubber bands and watching cartoons and eating cereal and microwavable meals while playing chess is childish anyway.

THE ONLY THINGS I'M BRINGING WITH ME TO SCHOOL tonight are Gio's friendship, my superpowers, and my Batman cape.

I don't leave a note for my mom, she'd only worry. She worries about me 86,400 seconds a day, and if she gets home before me, I don't want her calling me and interrupting my mission to conquer my fears of school, so I "accidentally" leave my cell phone on the kitchen table.

Then I lock the front door, which creaks like in a scary scene in a scary movie, and walk on my tiptoes so my neighbors don't hear my footsteps. If they can't hear me, they can't see me: my camouflage T-shirt makes me virtually invisible. Although I feel alive and popular, I am more anxious than usual. My left hand is glued to my nose, but the smell of my own skin isn't enough. That's why I'm wearing my blue, black, and yellow Batman cape. It makes me less invisible, but there's only a little bit of yellow on it, so given the time of day, I am as visible as a bat in a dark cave in a scary scene in a scary movie.

You're a bat, I tell myself, *a clean bat that just got out of a birth bath.*

Even though I'm a bat, walking seven-eighths of a mile in the dark isn't easy, so I close one eye and fly most of the way. I keep the other eye open so that I won't twist my ankle and fall in a puddle—again.

I pass the soaked baseball field, now caked in mud and old rain. Even if I tripped and tumbled into the deepest puddle on the infield, I wouldn't want to crawl into a ball and fall asleep. No, on this night I would get up.

Halfway to the school, I am glad for my camouflage shirt and bat speed because Beagle Eyes is still sitting in his chair at the gate of Clearview, squinting dangerously, but I am moving too fast and too invisibly for him to see me.

Sixty paces ahead, outside the new row of stores, the construction men, working into the night to finish building Starbucks, don't see me either. Their flashlights never once illuminate my Batman cape.

I continue on my journey, but it doesn't last long. Because of the speed of the flight, I arrive in 12 minutes and 23.6 seconds.

Radcliffe High School, home of the Mighty Jaguars. The school was built almost a hundred years ago, so it looks like a gray and black castle, sort of like the Batcave. The school colors aren't gray and black, though; they are orange and white. There are 1,528 students in the school if every single student comes, which will never happen because people get sick with the flu or mad at people or sad at people dying or happy for going to new places with their dads and therefore don't have to come to school.

Anyway, the parking lot, where I'm kicking only black

stones, is usually packed, but at night, it's pretty much naked. There are only three cars: a small blue one, a larger green one, and one black truck. I glance at my Batman watch. It's 8:14 p.m., and everyone knows that 13 is an unlucky number. If you're any good at math like I am, you know that $8+1+4=13$. I must wait until 8:15 before taking another step because the last thing I need tonight is bad luck.

There are clusters of fireflies everywhere, glowing then disappearing, but always visible to the trained eye. Since I have two trained eyes, I spot the fireflies hovering over wooden benches and the ones blinking in pine trees. In clumps, fireflies are easier to nab and cage and observe. But I don't want to. Not tonight.

Tonight I face my fears, which is one of the things the school psychologist, Ms. Adelman, has been trying to get me to do. If I can make it without being scared with no one around, maybe I can do it when class is in session. After all, Gio's got my back. That's what homies do, have each other's backs. It must be true because they say that in music videos.

It's now 8:15, and since $8+1+5=14$, not 13, I start walking again. There are three entrances to the school, each with four heavy doors. I'm approaching the student entrance. The four heavy doors are locked. I knew this would happen, that's why I brought a paper clip.

I've seen MacGyver do this hundreds of times. You stick the clip in the lock, twist the clip while scrunching your face, and then you hear a clicking sound and walk in.

I twist the clip and scrunch my face for twelve minutes

and three seconds—almost as long as my entire walk to the school—and then pound on the door with my fist until a flashlight blinds my eyes and almost ruins my new superhuman vision.

"What do you want?" a groggy voice asks.

It's the janitor, Mr. Traylor, a short man who wears a baseball cap every single day. As you could probably guess, he's wearing one tonight. It's a black hat with a bumblebee on it. The bumblebee looks friendly and familiar because, as I said, I love nature.

I wave my right hand from side to side and smile so that I, too, look friendly and familiar. "I accidentally left my notebook in my locker," I tell Mr. Traylor. "I need it for my English homework."

Lying is very easy for me, depending on who I'm talking to. For example, I don't tell people at school that I collect rubber bands after school. I say I go home to party.

"You only got ten minutes until I close up for the night," Mr. Traylor mutters.

"No problem," I say in my most laid-back, Will Smith–in-the-summer tone. "I'll be out in a jiff." Jif is my favorite brand of peanut butter.

I'm lying again, not about Jif being my favorite brand of peanut butter but about me leaving quickly. There's no way I can accomplish my mission in ten minutes.

As I wave goodbye to Mr. Traylor, he says, "Nice cape, kid" and laughs at me, not with me. I take it off until he is out of sight, and then of course I put it back on.

Radcliffe High School is pretty prestigious, at least that's what the principal wants everyone to think. That's why he put a trophy case twenty-four inches from the entrance. He figures that when students walk in, they'll inhale so much school pride that they'll do anything to add to the forty-two trophies for basketball, baseball, track, tennis, and math teams.

Imagine . . . kids busting their butts for a trophy only to see the principal ask for it back so *he* gets all the glory. It makes me sick and I want to throw up, but I don't, because if there's one thing I'm scared of it's throwing up. It saps your power to breathe and feels like a scary scene in a scary movie that you can't turn off even if you get too scared.

Anyway, alongside the trophies are plaques for teachers of the year. Mr. Head isn't one of them, which makes me feel sick again. As I bend over and hold my stomach, I spot a penny lying on the floor next to the trophy case. Abraham Lincoln's face is looking down at the ground instead of up at me. Obviously I don't pick it up because I need good luck tonight.

My locker's pretty close to the entrance, which is great because if anyone wants to talk with me when I walk in, I can say, "Sorry, got a date with my locker—and it's right over there."

Here, this is my locker. The combination is 17–29–37. On the top shelf are five notebooks my mom bought me for the first day of high school. They're in mint condition, not because I take extra special care of them but because I don't take notes.

I don't need to take notes because I trust my memory.

I know it's stupid not to take notes, but I do it anyway. I also know it's stupid to tap my locker with my left pinkie three times after I close it, but I do it anyway. No matter who is around, I give it three farewell taps with my left pinkie.

Above the lockers are posters for things separating the people on the outside from those on the inside: the math club, the football team, the dance team, and student government—as if it weren't hard enough fitting in with the Smartypants, Bigbulletholes, Angels, Cutters, Likegirls, and Devilblackcoats.

If it weren't for Gio, who obviously doesn't fit into any of these categories or else he wouldn't be best friends with me, I wouldn't like one single thing about school.

One of the posters above the lockers reads, "Don't like school? Vote for Bryan O'Toole." I think I'll vote for Bryan, even though his strawberry jelly belly would prevent me from taking him seriously.

Other than Bryan's poster, the words "club," "join," "dance," "event," and "fun" make me want to smell my left hand again.

I do. It smells like school, which smells like Old Spice deodorant, cologne, disinfectant spray, and fruity female hair sprays. I used to love the smell of fruity female hair sprays, especially in frizzy hair. But like mixing medicine with applesauce, all fruity female sprays are forever ruined because they've been contaminated with school.

The empty hallways, freshly mopped, lead to classrooms with large chalkboards and twenty-five seats with armrests attached. Teachers call those armrests "desks." They probably know it's stupid, but they, like me with my habit of tapping my locker three times with my left pinkie, do it anyway.

My favorite place in the school is Mr. Head's classroom, room 302. It's on the third floor. The steps, unlike tonight of course, are always packed. The rule is that you're supposed to stay on the right side. Students love breaking that rule, so I'm always afraid I'll fall or that someone will touch someone else by accident and I'll be blamed and beaten to a bloody pulp right on the staircase for everyone to see.

On the outside of Mr. Head's door is a sign: "Welcome to Success." Mr. Head's not a liar, but the sign is a lie. At least it is for me. How am I supposed to be a better writer than Phil if I still haven't learned how to write a poem, or a short story, or a novel, or even a journal entry? How am I supposed to keep track of my thoughts and record them if Mr. Head doesn't teach me?

Anyway, his door isn't locked.

Mr. Head's classroom is the best-looking one in the school. There are writing posters that my classmates and I made in purple marker, explaining rules on appositive phrases and semicolons and commas—and, of course, Mr. Head's golden rule about showing instead of telling. The golden rule is written in gold marker. I once helped Mr. Head hang up the golden rule poster when I didn't feel safe during lunch.

At the front of the room is a silver paper organizer that he calls "the bin," as in, "on your way out, put your homework in the bin." There is still a stack of papers in the bin. I grab the whole stack, which makes me feel like a teacher: you know, powerful, grown-up, and firm. My paper is the fourth one from the top: Rene. I don't write my last name on my papers because I don't like my last name. Fowler. It's a terrible last name because it's Phil's last name. Rene Fowler, it sounds like Phil owns me, that I belong to him, which I don't. So I only write Rene at the top of my papers. Besides, I'm the only Rene in my class. This is the only good thing about my name.

Another one of my papers is buried at the bottom of the pile. Mr. Head is about the slowest grader I've ever met. He's a good grader, though, because he's a teacher—not an exterminator. Exterminators look for grammatical errors and typos and liquidate them with their mighty red pens until every sentence is a bloody mess, and when I get my paper back, I think *I'm* a bloody mess, damned to hell for my sins. Teachers, however, kill only a few typos and explain what is good and what can be improved.

My papers aren't graded, so I put them back on top of the pile. Next to the papers is a journal. It's not a black-and-white composition book like all the students use for journal entries. You know, the ones in which you describe your book and write about a reading strategy, like visualizing or connecting. (I want to be a writer, I really do, but journal entries make me want to stab myself with my pencil instead of write with it because I can't jot my thoughts down fast enough.)

Anyway, this journal isn't anything like my black-and-white composition book. It's a brown leather journal that feels so soft that I want to pet it—and read it.

It's a new journal; I can tell because it makes a creasing noise when I open it. It's an adult's journal; I can tell because the writing is slanted and fancy.

Here, let me show it to you instead of telling you what it says:

September 20

I know I can do this. I just need to put my mind to it. In graduate school, they keep talking about how teenagers are resilient—well damn it so am I! I can be resilient, I know I can. Giovanni helped a great deal by calling me "brother man"—I don't know what it means but I like it—after I banged my head on the chalkboard. I can't believe I did that! But, damn, did it feel good! If you take it one day at a time, you can do it.

September 21

I can't do it. I'm living, breathing, and eating this job. Where has it gotten me? Sleepless nights. And loneliness: my oldest foe haunts me when I'm most vulnerable.

September 23

If I am humiliated any further, I'm outta here. I'll walk up to the front of the classroom—no, scratch that, I'll walk into the principal's office—and say, "Peace, I'm outta here." And if he doesn't like it, I'll say, "Listen, brother man. If you can't handle it, get off my biscuit." I don't know what that means either but I like it. Get off my biscuit. Release yourself from my biscuit. Leap off my biscuit.

Will anyone buy me a biscuit if I'm unemployed?

September 24

One week. That's all I'm giving you. If you don't see a dramatic change, I'm going to leave. I hate to be a quitter but . . .

It's not quitting. I'd simply be leaving one job and moving on to another. That should help you sleep tonight.

I drop the journal on the floor, but as I bend over to pick it up, I realize that even though Mr. Traylor, the janitor, cleaned the floors, there are always microscopic dirt and dust particles left behind, and since I don't want to leave my fingerprints anywhere, I use a tissue from Mr. Head's desk to pick up his journal.

After I return the evidence to its rightful place on Mr. Head's desk, I take three deep breaths like Ms. Adelman, the school psychologist, taught me, and *then* think.

I think the journal belongs to Mr. Head. I think the handwriting looks like Mr. Head's. I think Mr. Head is confusing his "I's" and "you's" and therefore is either a bad writer or has two guys wrestling in his head. I think Mr. Head thinks Gio is smart and that I am not. I think Mr. Head is going to quit. I think it is all my fault. I think Gio and I will have to save him. I think I can't take any more of this, at least not tonight.

I need to leave Mr. Head's room because my brain is pounding and I feel worse about myself. Besides, this isn't my mission tonight, and I'm not skilled at changing missions.

On the second floor, the lunchroom is completely naked. The only things that prove this is really the lunchroom I eat in every weekday and not some foreign movie set or rearranged dream are the food posters, including one of a food pyramid that I like because I like pyramids and because I like to see how many servings of each food group I get every day. Lucky Charms gives me multiple servings of both carbohydrates and sugar. Next to the food pyramid are posters telling students to "Vary Your Veggies"—whatever *that* means.

Other than those posters, the lunchroom, as I said, is naked. There aren't even any tables; they're all stacked up against the walls. It looks like one of those doomsday movies, where the day after doomsday, everything is naked and missing and deformed. I leave the lunchroom because I don't want to be a pond in a swamp. That's what Phil used to say, although I still don't know what that means.

The main office, also on the second floor, is locked—as is the guidance counselor's office. I was never afraid of those offices anyway, so I don't need to conquer my fear of them. I walk down the hall feeling light and unafraid, but as I approach the stairwell, my stomach does a belly flop. Radcliffe High School's gymnasium, like any other chamber of torture, is located in the basement.

My heart thumps louder and quicker with each one of the thirty-two steps I descend. I can already smell a fresh coat of wax on the polished floor. It may sound nice and clean—it may even *smell* nice and clean—but underneath, it's a bouquet of hairy armpits with no deodorant, and stale farts that got stuck on the walls. The most suffocating stench, though, is that of being alone.

A sparkling white and orange jaguar grins in the center of the court, surrounded by rows of bleachers unfolded, authentic, bone-chilling.

I feel dirty. I feel frightened. Most of all, I feel nauseous. I skipped my after-school cereal snack, which means that I haven't eaten since lunch, eight hours ago.

Those stupid butterflies in my stomach aren't flying anymore. They're dying. The taste of dying butterflies is too much to bear. I gag for seven seconds. My breath is stuck. So is my puke, which is a good thing because, as I've said, puking is like a scary scene in a scary movie that you can't turn off even if you get too scared.

But two seconds later, I gag again and this time orange and red chunks the size of small croutons spill from my mouth in an orange/brown soup. Two more gags follow, each producing less soup. The last heave tastes like peanut butter, which is a good thing, but there's barf on my shoes and puddles of puke on the freshly waxed floor.

And I'm crying. I can't help but cry when I throw up—like when it's so windy and cold outside that I can't block the wind or cold from clawing into my eyes and making my eyes leak.

I've had enough of stupid Radcliffe High School and its

stupid clubs and stupid cliques and stupid lockers and stupid lunchroom and stupid gym, and since my deodorant is wearing off and my sneakers smell like peanut butter and my mom should be coming home soon and I don't want her to worry, I walk down a pitch-black corridor to the student exit. I can already feel the fresh air that I'll need to fly through in order to get home before my mom does, so I adjust my Batman cape and sprint to the student doors and shove them—but go nowhere.

The doors are locked. With heavy chains.

No, can't be, I tell myself. It's only a joke that isn't directed at me, but with me. I just need to understand the joke.

"Mr. Traylor!" I yell, but all I hear back is the echo of my own pathetic voice. Breathe, I tell myself. This is only a movie. Will Smith is in it. It's very suspenseful and scary, but the good guy always wins.

Although the hallways are dark, I need to check the other doors, so I run to the other wing of the school, and I can feel my heart tapping and then knocking and then banging on my chest because I'm running fast, really fast, and I'm starting to realize that I could be stranded here, where I could die of hunger. And thirst. And shame. I realize that maybe a teacher is lying around somewhere, sleeping in a classroom or locker. In elementary school, I thought that teachers slept at school.

They don't. I am certain of that. None of the lockers open and all the classrooms on the first floor are locked.

I pass a fire alarm on the right side of the hallway and

think to pull it, but that would be breaking a law. I would be arrested and grilled by the Feds who would blow cigarette smoke in my face before they threw me in jail and put my face on the front of the newspaper for everyone to see, including my mom and Gio and Mr. Head.

The other doors don't budge. I take three deep breaths, like Ms. Adelman taught me, and *then* think. I think this is doomsday. I think I will not sleep tonight and will therefore turn into a zombie or a mummy—I hope just a zombie. I think that I must walk over to my locker and tap it with my left pinkie three times for good luck, and then check the last set of double doors.

I listen to my thoughts and reach the double doors. I push the heavy chains . . . I karate chop them . . . I kick them . . . I elbow them . . . I jump into them . . . but they are stone . . . and I am stuck.

And alone. I smell my left hand again and again as I sprint up the stairwell to check the windows on the second floor but the fall is too steep and jumping out of a building is no way to die a noble death, which is important in action hero movies like this one, so I run back downstairs and my heart is ready to explode, which would split open my sweat-soaked camouflage shirt that doesn't camouflage the tears snaking down my neck, because there's nowhere to go and nobody to help me and nobody to call. Call! I have no money or cell phone, but there's a pay phone near the lunchroom. I can call collect! Like on those old commercials!

Because pay phones are breeding grounds for dirt and

germs and ringworm, I pull my cape around my body and wrap it around the telephone. It makes me sad that I'll have to wash my cape when I get home—but I need to get home. "Rene," I say, when the friendly, lifesaving operator asks for my name. I've never loved my name more than I do now.

But my mom doesn't answer the stupid phone. It just rings and rings and then makes an *eh-eh-eh-eh* noise which sounds like my own scary scene in a scary movie that I need to stop because I don't want to be stranded and I don't want my mom to be missing—again. I take three deep breaths and *then* think. I think she's not home. I think she's not by herself because she's done that three times in the last two months. I think it was scary then, but this is doomsday.

I call back twenty-seven times, until I give up, walk back up to room 302, wipe the puke off my shoes with a tissue, and curl up like a ball on top of Mr. Head's brown desk.

The radiator crackles like distant fireworks. The floor creaks like an old rocking chair. A robber is trying to pick the lock on the student doors. He is wearing a black mask and has a steak knife tucked in the waist of his blue jeans. His smile is a jaggedly carved jack-o'-lantern and his chin is wet and sticky with pumpkin juice.

The robber has entered the building. I hold my breath so that he doesn't hear me. Footsteps approach the lunchroom. He will be disappointed that it is naked: no table, no food, no loot. He doesn't know that upstairs, the loot is in the form of a loser lying on a brown desk. Will he kidnap me for ransom or just kill me? Neither is a noble way to die.

His footsteps have disappeared. He must have removed his shoes. If he is barefoot, where did he put his shoes? Will the police find any evidence if I am taken hostage? They must, I decide. I reach into Mr. Head's drawer and pull out a paper clip. I ram it into my thumb until I draw blood. Fourteen drops fall onto the floor. That way, they'll be able to trace my DNA, and if they're any good at counting, they'll know how old I am—or was before my capture.

Now I must be a statue. No breathing, no clearing of the throat, no swallowing—and definitely no more thinking because, as Ms. Adelman once said, "Thoughts can be as loud as words."

The wind screams through the windows. Maybe it's Gio's voice, assuring me that any second now he will crash through the windows and whisk me away. I breathe in quickly through my nose, and then hold my breath again. I don't hear anything but that doesn't mean a thing. The robber could be outside Mr. Head's room, sharpening his steak knife.

My legs are shaking. I tell them to stop but they don't listen. I remain in a fetal position to preserve warmth for four minutes and thirty-two seconds until I realize I have a blanket.

I remove my Batman cape from my back and lay it across my chest so that I don't catch pneumonia, but if I do, and die from it, at least my cape will cover my body so that nobody at school will have to see me looking stupid and cold and dead and alone.

And responsible for Mr. Head quitting on us all.

"SOMEONE'S BEEN SLEEPING IN *MY* BED," SAYS A FAMILIAR voice.

I'm afraid to open my eyes, so I take three deep breaths and *then* think. I think I'm not dead. I think the robber either didn't exist or didn't find me. I think Mr. Head is talking to me. I think I'm sleeping on his desk. I think I must keep the journal a secret. I think my mom didn't come home last night. I think she knows that I didn't either. I think the sun already came up. I think it's safe to open my eyes.

"Good morning, Goldilocks," Mr. Head says. He's wearing a beige shirt and a green tie. "Did you eat all the porridge?"

He's laughing. I understand his joke, so I laugh, too.

Don't say anything about the journal, I tell myself. *Don't say anything about the journal. Don't say anything about the journal.*

I sit up and stare at my untied white shoelaces.

"I don't know what to say," I say instead of think.

"It's okay," he says. "You don't have to say anything. Although I don't know when you got here or why you're in school at, er, 6:08 in the morning, or what happened to you last night, but if it makes you feel any better, you should know that you're not the first one to sleep on that desk."

"Did Gio sleep on this desk?"

"No, Rene, Gio didn't sleep on this desk."

"Did Johnny Van Slyke sleep on this desk?"

"No, Rene, no students have slept on that desk."

"Then who?"

He sighs. "Me, Rene."

"But you're a teacher."

"Yes, Rene, I am."

"So it's true that teachers sleep at the school?"

"I . . . well . . . I guess, but I doubt anyone else does it. I, however, have slept on that desk too many nights to count."

Since I like to count and be exact, I say, "You can count, Mr. Head."

"I *can* count, Rene, but that doesn't mean I want to."

"Why not?"

"Because that would make me feel worse. Can you understand?"

"Yes, but why would you sleep *here*? It's cold and hard and lonely. Why would you want—"

Mr. Head's eyes get watery again, like they had during his hall duty after banging his head on the chalkboard—*this* chalkboard . . . I can touch it if I want to, but I don't want to because remembering bad memories can be almost as terrifying as the real thing. I don't want me or Mr. Head to remember bad memories.

"I've slept here, Rene, because, well, between you and me . . . I don't like school very much right now."

"I don't either!" I exclaim because I know that people who have things in common become friends.

"But you're a student, a teenager; you're not supposed to like school. I'm a teacher who gets paid to come here—who *chose* to come here—so I should like coming here, or at least be able to grin and bear it."

"But you're a *teacher*," I insist, "and teachers, as you probably know, have superpowers. They are smarter and stronger than everyone else." I elbow him in the arm and smile so that he doesn't think I'm trying to hurt him.

He only smiles a little bit. "Besides," I add, "if you didn't like school, you wouldn't be here so early."

He breathes in deeply and closes his eyes, which is a sign that a waterfall is about to explode in his eyes.

"I'm here early, Rene, because I need to prepare for the day's lessons. I need to plan and figure out how to be a decent . . . Look, do you promise to keep something a secret?"

I know he's talking about his journal, and I want him to be able to trust me, so I say, "You can trust me, Mr. Head. I won't tell anyone about your journal."

His right eyebrow twitches. "What did you just say?"

"I said, 'You can trust me, Mr. Head. I won't tell anyone about your journal.'"

"You—you read my journal?"

Although I'm good at lying, I'm not good at lying to Mr. Head, so I say, "Yes."

"Do you promise to keep that a secret?"

Because I'm still not good at lying to Mr. Head, I say, "No."

His eyeballs get bigger. "Why not?"

"Because I want to tell my friend, Gio." I love saying the words "friend" and "Gio."

"Gio? That's fine. Nobody else, though, okay?"

"Okay."

"Does anyone know you're here?"

"No."

"What—well, who do you live with?"

"My mom."

"You should call her. Do you want to use my phone?"

"No."

"Why not?"

"I called her last night. She wasn't home. She didn't come home last night."

"She . . . is she okay?"

"I don't know."

"Maybe you want to call her again?"

"Maybe I don't."

"Well maybe you should." He reaches into his pants pocket. "Here, use my cell phone."

"Just because I *should* call her doesn't mean I want to."

"Please, Rene, it would be really smart to call her."

Since I want to be smart (and want Mr. Head to *think* I'm smart), I grab his phone.

My mom sounds like she's been crying. In between sniffles, she promises to pick me up in two minutes. I say goodbye to

Mr. Head and shake his hand because he offers to shake mine.

I RUN INTO THE SHOWER AS SOON AS MY MOM PARKS THE car.

I wash my hands first, four times, so that I don't drag dirt over my body; hair is second because if I were to wash it last, the dirt from my hair would drip onto my newly clean body and ruin the shower; face is third; then I work my way down. At the end of the shower, I turn the water off only *after* I've positioned myself so that water won't drip on me as the stream weakens.

The water at the end of the shower is bad luck. When I turn off the shower, I don't want the end-of-shower bad-luck water to drip on my neck and shoulders because they'll be heavy from stress all day. I certainly don't want the end-of-shower bad-luck water to drip on my head because then my head and brain will be heavy from stress, which is the worst because if my head and brain are heavy from stress, then my neck and shoulders will be stressed, too, and if that happens, the stress works its way down. I don't want to start my day that way, especially after the way it's already gone. My mom and I didn't talk in the car on the way home, because we both knew each other's secrets, which created a lot of tension and stress, so I *really* didn't want to start off my day with end-of-shower bad-luck water.

"Rene! You need to hurry up!" I hear as I step out of the

shower. I'm mad at my mom for disappearing last night, so I ignore her.

The bathroom mirror is fogged up because very hot showers are one of my favorite hobbies. The bad part about this hobby is that foggy mirrors take a long time to become clear. You can wipe the mirror with your hand or towel, but it always leaves streaks and smudges that make you look deformed. Even I, who stand sixty-one inches tall and weigh ninety-seven pounds, end up looking fat and funky in a foggy mirror—like I have three eyes or two chins. This reminds me of a joke Phil used to say around fat guys: "He's got more chins than a Chinese phonebook." I hated when he said that because I knew it wasn't nice, but when I said that it wasn't nice, he would get angry and disgusted and roll his eyes and tell me I'd never get along with people if I didn't have a sense of humor.

Though I can't see myself very clearly in the foggy mirror, I know my buzz cut doesn't look like a buzz cut anymore, and I can tell that my lip fuzz is on its way to becoming a mustache, which is a very good thing because I once heard Gio say that "facial hair makes a man." That's why he changes his facial hair every week or so—from a mustache to a goatee to a beard to a soul patch. Since we're best friends, I hope he'll teach me how to grow hair on different parts of my face.

By the time I get out of the shower, get dressed, and eat my Lucky Charms, my mom is nervous. Really nervous. She's *always* nervous about being late. I hate being late, too—I mean, I *really* hate it—but my mission this morning is to make her angry. I am very skilled at this mission: I keep forgetting things from my room, I can't find my sneakers, I brush my teeth twice, I even floss my teeth.

"Please, hurry up!" she calls. I change my shirt. Three times. Too wrinkled. Too snug. Too shiny for a day on which I'm not feeling shiny.

Then I change my pants. Five times. The button is too loose. The zipper is stuck. There's an invisible stain on the right leg.

"What are you doing up there?" my mom yells.

"My pants smell like barf!" I shout. If she comes upstairs, I'll throw them into the hamper so that they mix with my old clothes and really *do* smell like barf.

"I'm getting tired of your game, Rene!"

I am, too. Even though I am succeeding at my mission, I'm sick of climbing into and out of my ugly clothes. I wipe the sweat from my face with my clean-but-soon-to-smell-like-barf pants, and toss them atop the mountain of clothes on the windowsill. The thought of putting on and taking off another article of clothing makes me feel sick and sweaty again, so I rest my forehead against the windowpane. It's freezing cold, which makes it easier for me to turn off my brain and stare out the window and count the number of seconds I can go without blinking.

Thirty-five seconds. But that was just a warm-up round. In round two, I last over a minute, which is my first great success today. "Something to build upon," that's what Ms. Adelman would say.

A small red car hums across the street. A man is reclining in the driver's seat. The back of his bald head faces me. He is getting balder every second that I stare at him (without blinking). Although I can't see his face, I am certain his eyes are closed, and that, like most balding men, his snores rumble like a loud burp. I write his story in my head: he had an awful day yesterday, almost as awful as mine. He overeats when he is stressed. Last night he ate seven bowls of Lucky Charms before he went to sleep. This made him snore. His wife tried shaking him. After eleven shakes, she smacked him in the face and told him to sleep in the car because, damn it, she has an important day ahead of her.

As I wave goodbye to the snoring man in the small red car, I hear my name stretched out longer than usual, "R e n e . . ."

It is not the snoring man. It's my mom. She doesn't say my name loudly, but there's an edge to her voice—like a man in a scary scene in a scary movie who says "H e l l o, p r e t t y" while holding an ice pick in his pocket. My mom doesn't stab me with an ice pick because she would never hurt me, but the way she says my name makes me move like my life depends on it.

By the time we get back in the car, my mom's breathing is loud and heavy. A minute later she's breathing even louder and heavier because of the traffic up ahead, which makes me happy because I am succeeding in my mission.

I'm so happy that I hum the song, "La Bamba," which is a Spanish song that I like to sing but *love* to hum because humming is a disguise for not knowing important things like the words. I'm so happy I even forget about sleeping on Mr. Head's desk last night. The happier I look, the angrier my mom looks.

She keeps tapping the steering wheel and sticking her head out the window while barking, "Damn it! It's 8:39! Damn it! Damn it! Damn it to hell!"

The cars ahead of us look parked. She takes a deep breath and says, "Rene," which is a sign she wants to talk to me about something serious. "Please tell me where you were last night."

"No."

"I'm your mother," she says, which is a stupid thing to say because we've both known that for fourteen years. "I worry about you."

In order to make her angrier, I say, "Mom, I'm your son. I worry about *you*."

"Look, Rene, I'm sorry I was late last night . . ." I look out the window and fold my arms against my chest, but she continues anyway: "Sometimes life can be so . . . stressful and . . . overwhelming . . . that I feel like I'm . . . drowning, so sometimes I need a break . . . to come up for air, you know?"

"No."

"I'm sorry, Rene," she says, trying to unfold my arms. I want her to know I'm still mad, and that I'll *still* be mad when I get home from school. Phil used to tell me not to hold grudges, but I was invisible when he said that.

"Finally, the damn traffic is moving," my mom says, brushing back her hair as she peeks at herself in the mirror.

I ignore her because although I have succeeded in my mission, I don't feel I have.

One minute and seventeen seconds later, we've arrived at Radcliffe High School. I open the car door and don't say goodbye. I walk quickly to the front entrance.

Everyone knows.

Everyone knows I was here when they were sleeping in their own houses in their own warm beds.

That's all I keep thinking as I open the heavy doors. Thankfully, the janitor isn't at the entrance. Before he shows up and announces to the whole school that I'm a loser who wears capes and sleeps on desks, I scurry down the hallway. First, I stop at my locker to see if I left any incriminating evidence linking me to last night's crime, but the locker looks as innocent as I look guilty.

Then I remember the puke. It's still on the gymnasium floor! The last thing I need is for the gym teacher to report suspicious activity to the police, who will call their forensic specialists, who will do DNA testing on it and tell the Feds to book me for trespassing. So I sprint down the hallway and grab a roll of toilet paper from the bathroom and then run to the staircase. I can smell it from the top of the steps but I need to keep going so I race down the staircase and see that it's still there. All of it.

Nobody has gym first period, so it's just me and my bodily waste. Gagging, I use the whole roll of toilet paper to mop it up but I don't touch it with my hands; I drag it with my sneakers and use them to hoist it into the trash can.

Satisfied, I walk back to my locker. After I unload two textbooks I obviously didn't read the night before, I hear one

Devilblackcoat say to another Devilblackcoat that she's tired. The other Devilblackcoat laughs because it's an inside joke about me sleeping at the school.

One Cutter says to a Bigbullethole that he didn't go to English class because it's always cold in Mr. Head's room. The Bigbullethole laughs because it's an inside joke about me using my Batman cape as a blanket.

One Smartypants says to another Smartypants, "The referee screwed up royally. It was *obviously* a foul," which is an inside joke about how I, Rene Fowler, am so screwed up, so royally screwed up, that I puked on the gym floor.

My face is crimson by the time one Likegirl says to a Cutter that he, like, is her, like, hero, which is an inside joke about me thinking that I had superhuman vision—but didn't, which is why I couldn't see Mr. Traylor chain the doors before I could escape.

I slam my locker shut and then tap it three times with my left pinkie in order to change my luck. I wish Ariel were here, but this isn't a day for red roses. They would look and smell too out of place—like seeing an orange beach ball and smelling coconut sunblock at a funeral.

My Batman watch says that it's 8:57, which isn't an unlucky number but I don't want to walk into first period with only three minutes left because the people will hiss to each other like rattlesnakes about what I did and where I slept; and if the teacher gets distracted when someone knocks on the door to talk about report cards or a Cutter or an upcoming fire drill, everyone in the class will fall off their chairs, pointing and laughing at me until I run into the halls, where I am right now anyway, so I plan on roaming the hallways for three minutes until the bell rings.

The hallways look prettier during the day. The activity posters look brighter, the floors shinier, the lunchroom more fully clothed. There are two minutes until the bell when time stands still.

Gio is walking down the hall, his curly hair bouncing with each confident stride. He doesn't notice me; he keeps bopping down the hall, king that he is. Are we not friends? Does he have too many friends? Does *everyone* call him "Gio"? He's going to pass me. I clear my throat and think of how to talk to a friend.

I know what being cool sounds like. I've tried to talk like everyone else by using phrases like, "What up?" "What's up?" "Tzup?" "How's it goin'?" "What's goin' on?" "What's good?" . . . but it feels artificial. And people laugh. I prefer to say "Hi," and if I'm feeling as loose and relaxed as Will Smith, I say, "Hey."

"Hi, Gio," I say, waving.

"Oh, hey brother man, what's shakin'?" he says, reaching out to give me something in between a handshake and a high five.

He gives up when he realizes I'm not moving my hand. He nods toward the clock on the wall and asks, "You just got here?"

"No," I tell him.

"You're cutting, too?" he says, punching me in the arm.

"I am NOT a Cutter," I blurt out, then realize that Gio and

I will never be friends because Cutters can only be friends with other Cutters, Bigbulletholes, or Likegirls. Since I am *in between* those groups, there is no hope.

Just in case I'm wrong, though, and don't spend the next year of my life picking rubber bands off the dark streets for no reason, I ask, "Are you a Cutter?"

"I cut," he says. "But I'm not a Cutter."

In my head, I am dancing to and humming the song, "La Bamba."

But Gio looks mad. "Man, kids in this damn school—and I see you've been sucked in, too—get so caught up in their damn groups. It's like they don't even know who they are anymore; they simply do what the group says they should do; wear what the group says they should wear. They *must* do it, or else they don't even recognize themselves. I don't buy into it—any of it: groups, clothes, electronics—brother man, I've boycotted *cell phones* just to be different. I still have friends, though, don't get me wrong, people know me—I mean it's pretty hard not to notice my Afro bouncing down the hall—but at the end of the day, when the sun sets and the crickets sing, I know who I am, so the last thing I need is to be labeled something as meaningless as a Cutter."

I don't know he is finished because "La Bamba" is still playing in my head, but then I notice that Gio is staring at me, and since I know it would be inappropriate to hug him and call him my long lost brother, I talk about small things.

"How often do you cut class?" I ask.

He shrugs. "From time to time. The teachers are all right,

but it's such a drag living the same day over and over, you know?"

"You have no idea," I tell him.

"Well, cutting once in a while breaks up the monotony."

"Gio!" a loud familiar voice shouts down the hallway. It belongs to the man who, other than Mr. Traylor, I dread the most today.

"Oh, good morning, Mr. Head," Gio says, sounding chummy.

"Come on over here for a minute, Gio." Mr. Head is still in his beige shirt and green tie. There are dark puddles of sweat under each of his arms. I am responsible for those puddles.

Gio excuses himself and jogs over to Mr. Head, who doesn't even look at me. I throw my hood over my head so that I become invisible, and sneak around the corner. Luckily, the bell rings. Above the buzz of students hustling to their next class, I can tell that Mr. Head isn't happy because he is using the same words and tone that my mom always uses. "Why would you do that?" he asks, looking disappointed. "What were you *thinking*?"

"I don't know what you mean, sir," Gio says.

"Don't play dumb with me, young man. You were cutting again weren't you?"

"Yes, I was."

"How many times have we talked about this?"

"This is our fifth time, sir."

"*Fifth time!* When will you *get it*?"

"I know I shouldn't have cut again, Mr. Head, sir, but I needed to canvass for New Jersey's Democratic Party, sir."

"Canvass?"

"Well, with the election coming up next month, the Democrats need as much help as they can get. Voters—and, as you know, there are plenty of seniors in this school who can vote—need a firm grasp of the issues before they close that curtain and vote. An ignorant voter is a Republican voter, that's what my mom always says. As we speak, my mom is canvassing in my neighborhood, which has leaned Republican for decades, but given the shift in demographics over the past few years, I think we have a shot. But we need leadership. If not me, then who? If not now, then when? You taught us that, sir."

Mr. Head's face softens. "I did?"

"Well, sure. When we were reading my now-favorite book, *The Count of Monte Cristo,* you explained that Edmond's community lacked strong leadership. That's why corruption was able to overrule Monsieur Morrel's dying pleas for Edmond's release."

"I—I taught you that?"

"A society without leadership is a breeding ground for lawlessness and irresponsibility."

"I taught you *that,* too?" A smile forms at the corner of Mr. Head's mouth.

"Yes, sir. You've been a beacon of hope for the entire freshman class. They don't always express it, but you know how teenagers, especially freshman, can be: always drinking that Haterade."

"Yes! They do! They're always drinking the—anyway, well, keep up the good work, Gio. My girlfriend, er, 'female companion,' serves on the Democratic board of directors at the state level. We all try to do our part. That's kind of why I got into education in the first place—for better or worse."

Gio pats him on the shoulder. "Trust me, it's for the better, sir."

"Um, well, thank you." Mr. Head clears his throat. "Good talk . . . but I better not catch you cutting English class, you hear?"

"Wouldn't miss it for the world, sir."

"Well, then, carry on. You don't want to be late for next period."

I do, but first I need to know how Gio did this—whatever *this* was. As soon as Mr. Head is out of earshot, I nod at Gio.

He's smiling proudly, but I speak first. "How did you—"

"Do that? I'll tell you later," he says. "I've got a question for you first. If you didn't, as you said, just arrive at school, and you weren't cutting, what were you doing?"

"I had a sleepover at the school."

"With a girl?"

"No."

"By yourself?"

"Yes."

"That's b'noodles!"

"Which means uniquely cool," I tell him.

He laughs. His chipped tooth winks at me. "Which class do you have next?"

"History with Mr. Chalmers."

"Then you better go," he says. "Besides Mr. Head's class, Mr. Chalmers's class is the only one I never miss."

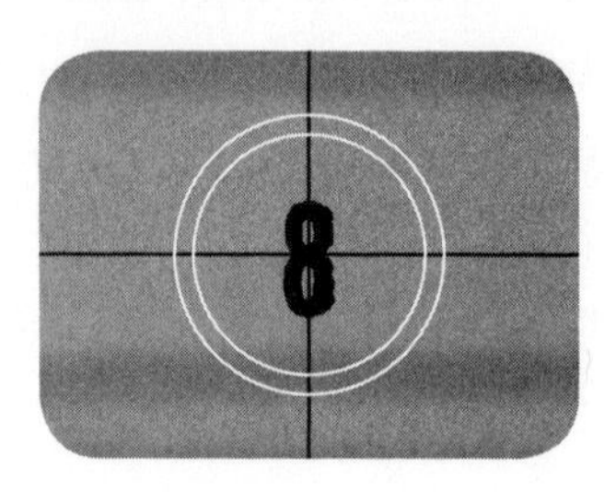

REMEMBER I TOLD YOU HOW NOBODY LISTENS TO MR. Head? That's because nobody even *breathes* in Mr. Chalmers's class.

Mr. Chalmers is even taller than Giovanni—and much thicker. Although I love nature, I'm no expert on trees, so I can't tell you which tree Mr. Chalmers most resembles, but he looks like a really strong tree, and his voice sounds like the deep echo you'd hear if you shouted into the trunk of that really strong tree.

Every time I'm in his class I want to smell my left hand, but I can't because my hands are always pressed together like I'm in church, praying that God doesn't smite me.

In room 116, Mr. Chalmers *is* God. He actually said that.

On the first day of school, while pacing up and down *his* aisles, he said, "Now I want to be very clear. This is not a democracy. This is a dictatorship. And I am Caesar. If you don't feel comfortable calling me Caesar, I understand. You may call me God. Otherwise, it's Mr. Chalmers. Not, 'Yo, Mr.' or 'Hey, Chalmers.' For the next nine months, you will be in labor. Hard labor. Homework every night, silence every class period, lectures that demand furious note taking. There will be no movie breaks, no off-days, no substitutes, no review sheets. If you want help, pray to God. Or ask me. Same thing."

Nobody cuts Mr. Chalmers's class. Nobody talks back or out of turn. Nobody clears his throat or sneezes without catching it in a tissue. Because Mr. Chalmers has eyes in the back of his head. He pounces on you like waiters refilling glasses of water at a Chinese restaurant, except he doesn't bring water; he brings pain—to your grade and your ego and your eardrums.

I'm pretty sure Mr. Chalmers was in the marines because on the first day of school, he said, "I was in the marines. So watch yourself."

Plus, Mr. Chalmers looks like Popeye—without the pipe, the tattoos, or the sailor hat. And he's not bald. He's young, maybe twenty-eight years old. The Likegirls both fear and, like, love him; the guys fear him but don't love him. I'm a guy, as I've said, so I only fear him.

But fear alone can't make me pay attention, because fear alone is overrated—like Phil and his $2 bills. For instance, the other day Mr. Chalmers talked about Franklin Delano Roosevelt's famous line, "The only thing we have to fear is fear itself," but I don't remember anything about Franklin Delano Roosevelt except that stupid quote, because every five seconds, Mr. Chalmers sniffled. He didn't even have a cold or a hanging boogie. I know what sniffling a boogie sounds like. It sounds like drinking through a straw when there's barely any soda left. Mr. Chalmers's sniffles sound like *blowing* through a straw when you don't have *any* soda left.

And he does it every single class—every ten seconds. On most days, I give up trying to pay attention and instead tally how many times he sniffles in the hour-long period. If you're any good at math, like me, you could calculate it. The answer is 360 sniffles, which makes it impossible to concentrate. Listening to Mr. Chalmers is like the whisper-down-the-lane game. You know, where one person tells someone something and then that person tells someone else until eventually the message gets all jumbled. Here, let me show you:

Mr. Chalmers: "Get this down in your notebooks: The Great Depression impacted millions of people because jobs were cut; therefore, families, especially fathers, were under a tremendous amount of pressure."

Me: Okay, Rene, you don't need to write it down; all you have to do is remember that the Great Depression impacted millions of people because jobs were cut, so fathers felt pressure.

Mr. Chalmers: (sniffle)

Me: That makes 140 sniffles already and we're only twenty-four minutes into the class! I think he's on pace to break his record.

Mr. Chalmers: (sniffle)

Me: That's 141! I should calculate if he's on pace to break his record.

Mr. Chalmers: (sniffle)

Me: Another one! Wait, what was Mr. Chalmers saying?

Oh, right, that there are millions of great people who are depressed and therefore cut themselves because of pressure to impress their fathers.

The whisper-down-the-lane game will get even harder today because everyone will be whispering about me. I enter Mr. Chalmers's room like a silent statue. Because of the silence in his class, I can't hear anyone's whispers, but their eyes, their smiles, their looks . . .

Instead of counting Mr. Chalmers's sniffles, I count the seconds I have left until I must face Mr. Head and the hissing rattlesnakes in his poisonous class.

DOOMSDAY. I AM LEAVING DEATH ROW. NEXT STEP: MY EXecution. I trudge to Mr. Head's room, shuffling my feet. The shackles on my wrists and ankles clang with each step. There are smirks on everyone's faces. Some at least look away, but most of them don't. Their eyes say, "You're getting what you deserve. I hope you rot in hell."

When I walk into Mr. Head's room, two Smartypants kids (Johnny Van Slyke and his friend, Norman), one Likegirl, and one Devilblackcoat hiss their rattlesnake hisses and flash their rattlesnake eyes at me. It can't be mistaken for anything but an inside joke about the desk I fell asleep on a few feet away from them.

Their rattlesnake jaws widen as I find my seat. Johnny Van Slyke's purple polo shirt is so small that his biceps are breaking through the thin fabric. He looks like Arnold Schwarzenegger before he became governor.

I take out my notebook and pen, but I have no intention of writing anything. I can't focus on becoming a better writer than Phil because I must divide my radar between the rattlesnakes and a sweating Mr. Head, who is scribbling notes on the board about dramatic irony.

"Okay, listen up," he says. "For those in the back who can't read my awful handwriting, it says here that dramatic irony is a literary element that many authors use in order to create tension. It occurs when the reader knows something about a character that other characters don't know."

I look down at my empty notebook so that the rattlesnake venom doesn't poison me. Mr. Head smiles. Even *he* is in on the joke. Everyone thinks they know something that I don't. They don't think I know that they know. I know!!! I turn off the noise by putting my hands over my ears. I try to hum "La Bamba," but the rattlesnake noises are too loud. I take three deep breaths, and when I look up twelve seconds later, nobody is looking at me.

Everyone is staring at Johnny Van Slyke, who is banging his fist on his desk.

"WHY NOT?!" Johnny thunders in Mr. Head's direction.

"Because you've already gone to the bathroom, Johnny." Mr. Head sounds like he's talking to an infant—or me. Mr. Head's armpit puddles are growing.

"BUT I GOTTA GO AGAIN!"

"Well, you'll have to hold it like Vicky and Gina and Louis"—Vicky and Gina and Louis stare daggers at Mr. Head—"and anyone else who has already gone."

Johnny snorts. "You don't *know* who else has gone to the bathroom? You really *don't know*?"

Mr. Head doesn't know; that's why he closes his eyes. "Look, Johnny, I've got to get through this lesson. I spent two hours preparing this morning"—*Please don't tell everyone about this morning. Please don't tell everyone about me sleeping here*—"planning for this lesson and I need to get through it."

"But *I* don't," Johnny hisses. "All *I* gotta do is get through this stupid discussion so that I can leave. Wait, I actually don't. I can leave with or without your permission. I'm about to dip. I'm outta here."

Mr. Head turns his back to the class and taps the chalkboard with a tiny piece of white chalk. I know his fist is clenched because I can see three blue veins snaking up his right hand. "Anyway," he says. His voice is shaking. "Dramatic irony is used to—"

"Forget this chump," Johnny mumbles to his friend, Norman, and pushes his chair out. "I'm gonna go. I'm gonna dip because Head ain't gonna tell *me* what to do." Johnny stands up. "See you later. I'm out."

Mr. Head turns around and says, "Well, you keep talking about it . . . why don't you just *leave* already?" He smirks, and everyone, especially me, smirks with him.

"I *will* leave," Johnny says, walking toward the door. "See ya, suckers."

"Very mature, Johnny," says Mr. Head. "Thank you for coming today."

Get 'em, Mr. Head. Get 'em.

The snake look returns to Johnny's eyes. "Maybe I won't leave. You know, maybe I'll just"—he reaches for the light switch and sings—"turn the lights off, turn the lights off . . . ta—ta—turn the lights off . . . ta—ta—turn 'em off . . ."

The class is silent. So is Mr. Head. He doesn't move a muscle. Maybe it's the lights, but he doesn't even blink. He looks dead, the life sucked out of his sweaty face.

As Johnny flips the lights on and off, some invisible switch within me that I never knew existed flips on. My nostrils flare. My eyes widen. My hands shake. The muscles in my legs tighten.

I've seen enough superhero movies to know that adrenaline flows fastest in the dire moments. Batman nabbed the Joker as he stared death in its pale face. Spider-Man saved his beloved Mary Jane by flinging the quickest, most accurate web with not a second to spare. Superman lifted a car.

I lift my desk. And flip it upside down.

"LEAVE ALREADY!!!" a voice I recognize as my own booms. "GET THE FUCK OUT OF MR. HEAD'S ROOM!"

Mr. Head's eyes pop out of his head. "Rene! You don't need to—"

"GET OUT!"

As Johnny hesitates, that voice snaps again, "GET OUT! NOW!!!"

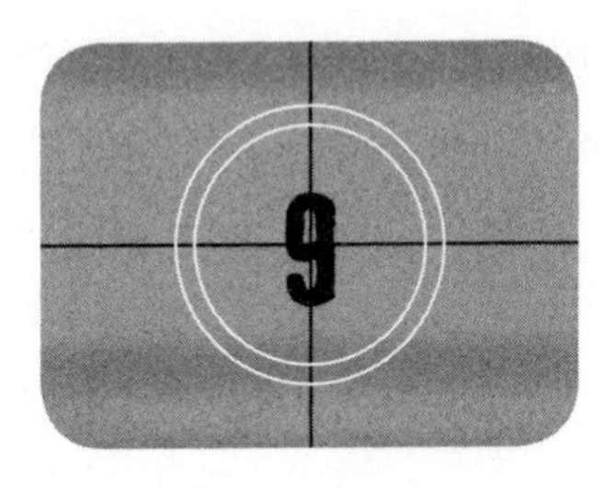

THE BELL RINGS. EVERYONE, EXCEPT ME, IS FREE AND HAPPY and can go home and smile and watch television and collect bugs and eat cereal.

But I am dead.

Johnny Van Slyke is waiting for me. Everywhere. He is hiding behind the school trophy case. He is lurking outside the lunchroom. He is beside me, hissing in my ear.

I dash down the hall and kick open the doors. The sun is blinding.

My eyes bounce from side to side, scanning the crowd for my executioner. I don't see him, but that doesn't mean he's not here. He could be wearing someone else's clothes; he could've stolen someone else's voice like Ursula did from Ariel in *The Little Mermaid*; he could've carved someone's face off and stuck it on his own.

And then it happens. Behind me, a male voice. "I knew I'd find you here."

Doomsday.

"So you said, 'Get off my biscuit,' and he . . . left?"

It's Gio's voice, but it could be Johnny Van Slyke using

Gio's voice, so I try to think of a question only Gio would know the answer to, but I haven't told him my secrets yet, so I ask, "When you met me yesterday, what did I fall in?"

"What?"

A school bus honks at another school bus. One of the drivers yells, "Move your bus or I'll move it for ya!"

"You heard me," I tell Johnny Van Slyke/Gio. "When you met me yesterday, what did I fall in?"

"Why are you—"

"Just answer the question!" I bark at Johnny Van Slyke/Gio.

"A puddle, why?"

I take a long, deep breath.

"So you said, 'Get off my biscuit,' and he just left?"

"No," I explain.

"Well, what'd you say?"

"Get out NOW."

"And he left?"

"Yes." I don't want to use too many words because I'm out of breath. My voice and knees are shaking. I want to lift more desks or cars, but there's a slight tremor in my left hand. When I try to smell it, it bumps into my lips.

"I'm speechless," he says.

I smile. "B'noodles, huh?"

"Definitely. You got caught in a pickle jam so you spilled your wrath."

"Yup."

"You got all swollen like the Hulk, flexed your muscles and roared."

"Yup," I say, but what I don't tell him is that I am scared I will jinx myself by being overconfident and boastful. At church, the preacher is always talking about how God rewards humility over arrogance. Plus, whenever I am *really* happy about something, the happy thought transforms into an unhappy thought that makes me unhappy.

"I don't quite know how to ask this," Gio says, "so I'll just ask it."

"Ask what?"

"Why?"

"Why what?"

"Why pop your lid for Mr. Head?"

"I had to."

"I don't get it."

Since I already told Mr. Head that I would, I say, "Gio, I want to tell you everything but I—"

"But what?"

"But I need to breathe first."

One minute and thirty-two seconds later, I tell him everything: fireflies, caterpillars, superhuman vision, my missions, Batman, the journal, Mr. Head's desk.

And then, it's over. *We* are over.

I've scared him away. The insane, freaky kid shows how insanely freaky he is and the sane, mature, young man shows how rational he is by doing what is best for him. It's inevitable, bound to happen by the laws of nature. If everyone is allergic to me, why shouldn't he be, too?

He sticks his hand in the air and spreads his fingers, the

international signal for farewell, adios, have a nice life. He is moving far away from me for a long, long time, maybe forever, depending on whether or not I end up in the tenth grade or locked up like the Joker in Gotham's Arkham Asylum with shackles around my wrists and ankles so that someone can shower me instead of allowing me to complete my hair-to-toes routine.

"This means that you're supposed to—" he starts, but I don't want to hear him say it, so I finish the sentence for him, "—disappear," I say. "Leave town. Get a life, but don't share it with anyone else so they don't get contaminated." I throw on my hood so that I'm invisible.

He points at his fingers. "High-five," he says, "that's what this means."

"Oh." I give him a high five.

"Now let's continue your mission of saving Mr. Head from himself."

I take off my hood so that I'm not invisible anymore; I want the world to see me in all my glory. But then I remember that Johnny Van Slyke could still be at school and looking for me. I throw my hood back on.

"See you tomorrow," Gio says. He pats me on my right shoulder and walks past me.

Tomorrow! What if I'm not alive tomorrow! What if Johnny nabs me on my way home and beats me to a bloody pulp until I am unrecognizable and won't be identified for hundreds of years until a new generation of white-bearded archaeologists dig the earth for dinosaur fossils and find me instead?

I don't want to put Gio in danger, but I ask him anyway. "Can—can we walk home together?"

"Not going home," he says. "Sorry, brother man."

Say something! Tell him you need his help! Tell him you won't see him tomorrow unless you speak up! SPEAK UP!

"You all right, brother man?"

"Sure, sure. I'll be fine."

"Look, you wanna come with me?"

"Okay!" I blurt out. "I like it there!"

He chuckles. "I didn't even tell you where I'm going."

"Oh, I—"

"I'm going to a nursing home."

Night of the living dead . . . walking skeletons, rattling bones, white sheets, and soiled diapers . . . nurses with needles and red eyes holler at three-foot ladies, "Soon you'll be going to sleep for a long, long time—so you better practice tonight! Lights out!"

"Rene—yo, Rene." Gio is shaking me. "You look like you saw a ghost."

"I did."

He laughs. "Have you ever been to a nursing home?"

"No."

"You should."

"What do you do there?"

"I visit old people."

"Are your grandparents there?"

"Not anymore. They're dead."

"So why do you—?"

He closes his eyes, which means that he is either annoyed with me or upset about old people. I ask if he's annoyed with me.

"It's not you," he says. It must be the old people, and since everyone knows that dying is the thing old people are most famous for, I ask if he's upset about his grandparents dying.

He closes his eyes again, but this time he speaks: "You know how in middle school, when cliques are forming and your circle of friends, friends you've had since you were two or three, split down the middle and run away from each other as if a flaming stick of dynamite were thrown at them?"

I nod.

"Well, that stick of dynamite that separated everyone, it had a name—it *still has* a name—but I don't care about it anymore. You know what I'm talking about? You know its name?"

I shake my head because I don't know the names of any superheroes who use dynamite.

"Popularity," he says. "My grandparents were five minutes away from me, but I visited them only a few times a year. I wanted to be popular—and visiting grandparents wasn't exactly the best strategy. So I ignored them. Pretended they weren't alive. And soon enough, they weren't."

He sighs. "I know I didn't shorten their lives or anything, but I could've done so much more. I could've—"

I look at my shoelaces. They are gray.

“Sorry to lay all this on you,” he says, running his hand through his mop of curly hair. “I feel like I can talk to you, like you don’t judge me. You don’t care about being popular. I like that.”

Since I don’t know what to say, I don’t say anything.

“Look, you wanna come or what?”

My mom always said helping old people makes you feel better (or at least less lousy) and since I need to feel less lousy about Johnny Van Slyke and my imminent death, I decide to go. I want to play it cool, like a friend, a cool friend, so I say, “I guess I’ll go.”

“I *guess* I’ll go,” he chuckles as we head toward the home of old people.

"I can't wait for you to meet them," Gio says, as we approach McNaughton's Nursing Home.

I want to tell him that we shouldn't wait because time is running out and they could be dead by the time we get there. Instead, I say, "Yeah, it should be fun."

At the corner of the wheelchair ramp, I spot a shiny coin. I bend over and pretend that I am tying my shoes. It's a quarter. I can see George Washington's face, so I put it in my pocket.

"Ready?" Gio asks.

He holds the door for me as I hold my breath. The lobby doesn't look that bad: two receptionists with red lipstick wish us a good afternoon. Framed pictures of nature—the Jersey shore and Pine Barrens—convince me that I might have been wrong about nursing homes.

Until we reach the hallway. So this is what I have to look forward to if I survive Johnny Van Slyke . . . A lady in a white dress pushes a vacuum along a faded brown carpet. Yellow hallway lights buzz. White walls smell of dirty underwear. Muscular Jamaican men in tank tops turn old ladies in their beds.

In the middle of the hallway, dressed in green flannel shirts, wrinkled men read yesterday's news. "Time for the bathroom, sir," a nurse calls. A man shifts in his wooden seat and reaches for his steel walker. His arms shake like branches in a storm as he climbs upright. I think of making up his story like I did for the bald, snoring man in the small red car outside my window, but it'd probably be too depressing. The man catches his breath and steadies himself before shuffling his feet to the bathroom. I don't know whether he means to or not—maybe he's doing it to save time in the bathroom—but his pants are falling down. His spotted butt looks like chopped liver. With each step he takes, he farts. Loudly. The rumble follows the naked man to the bathroom.

I want to wash my hands, over and over again, but not in *that* bathroom.

"Rene, over here," Gio calls.

The exit behind me is only twenty-eight paces away. I scribble a note in my mind to escape if I see any more butt cracks.

"Brother man, come on, what are you *doing*?"

I shuffle my feet down the hall. I'm fitting in already.

Gio points at two old people playing cards. The woman is in a wheelchair; the man sits in a wooden chair with a gray walker at his side. They don't look up until Gio says, "Playing casino, *again*? What happened to spit and spades and the other games I showed you?"

"How nice to see you, dear," the old woman says.

"Nice to be seen."

"How's my boy?" the old man says, dropping his cards.

Gio grins. "I'm good."

The man scrunches his fleshy face. "*Good?* After teaching me all those expressions you boys use these days, you tell me you're *good*? Are you feeling, um, what's that dang—oh, are you feeling b'noodles, my boy?"

Gio laughs. "You don't *feel* b'noodles. You *are* b'noodles. Get it?"

"Got it."

"Good." Gio turns to me. "Rene, this is Milton and this is Edith."

Since everyone loves compliments, even old people, I tell them I like their names. Edith, in a yellow silk blouse, thanks me by touching my forearm with her left hand. I wonder if this is how old people high-five each other.

"Feel like getting some air, fellas?" Milton asks. "It smells like a stale fart in these hallways."

"I know who did it," I blurt out, still hearing the naked man's rumble.

Milton coughs into his palm. "Try to find someone who *doesn't* cut the cheese around here. Even Edith lets one go every now and then."

"Oh, Milton!" Edith says, slapping him on the shoulder.

"Don't deny it, you *do*."

Milton must be telling a joke because everyone knows girls, especially old ladies, don't fart. It's safe to laugh, so I do.

"Damn, this kid *loved* that one," Milton says. "What's your name again, boy?"

"Rene," I tell him.

"Names these days!" he chortles. "I almost married a Rene."

Even though he's making me laugh, I am glad he didn't marry me.

"So, you boys ready for some fresh air?"

Gio nods, so I do, too.

"Upseedaisy," Milton grunts, pulling himself up by his walker. His lumberjack hands are all veins.

"Come on, Edith, I'll race you. Last one outside is a rotten egg! And don't even *think* about cheating again; Giovanni is *not* allowed to push you. You know the rules."

"I know," she says. "No cheating with Giovanni."

"Ready, set, go!" Milton cries, shuffling forward. "And we're off, like a toupee in a windstorm!"

Edith spins her wheelchair, eyes peeled on the finish line at the end of the hall.

The soundtrack of McNaughton's Nursing Home gets louder with each move they make: "*You* don't have Bingo. *I* have Bingo." . . . "That stupid manager should'a pulled that pitcher in the second inning. He had nothing left. *Nothing.* Imagine if he had to face Mays or the Duke—or the Mick! Now *those* guys were good" . . . "The red pills are for my liver. The blue pills are for my ulcer. The white pills are for my arthritis. I don't know what those brown pills are for" . . . "I'm telling you, the president's a shyster, a good-for-nothing hope salesman. My father was a salesman, a liquor salesman who loved liquor. He would've made a terrible president" . . . "Eight ball, corner pocket. You better pay up. And there she falls. A pack of candy in *my* corner pocket . . ."

Five minutes into Milton and Edith's race, we are almost at the front door. Twenty more paces to go. Gio shouts into his fist as if it were a microphone. "And . . . down . . . the . . . stretch . . . they . . . come!"

For the first time in my life, I feel like a hare, watching two tortoises crawl to the finish line: Milton, hunchbacked and breathing hard, makes "ooooWEEE" noises each time he moves his walker; Edith, two feet in front of Milton, is curled up in her wheelchair, her chin on her chest. With three paces to go, they are dead even until Milton stops, grunts loudly, looks to his right, bends slightly at his waist and says, "Ladies first."

Gio holds open the door as Edith exits the building. As Milton follows her out, he grabs Gio by the arm. "Taking notes, boy, on how to be a gentleman?"

"Yes, sir," Gio says.

"Good. Now, do yourself a favor and take better notes in school. Gotta bring up those grades, you hear?"

"Oh goodness!" Edith cries. "How beautiful!" The sunset is an oil painting with purple, pink, and red splashed across the sky. "Can you *imagine* how beautiful the garden must look at this hour?"

The nursing home's garden is just down the block. My

head feels lighter as we sit down and stare at a bed of orange daisies. The orange flowers remind me of Ariel, which makes my head even lighter. If I were a bee, I would eat only from orange daisies. "Angel flowers," that's what they should be called. They should sell them as "Angel flowers" at the local flower shop. I bet the owner would make enough money to open another flower shop, which of course he'd name *Ariel* because she's—

Milton must have superpowers, like most old people do, because he leans forward and whispers, "My boy . . . you're in love, aren't you?"

"No," I lie.

"Did anyone ever tell you you're a terrible liar?"

"No," I lie again.

"You go to Gio's school?"

I nod.

"Both you fellas like the same girl?"

I check to see if my Ariel is swimming in Gio's eyes. I don't *think* I see her, but that doesn't mean she's not there.

Edith touches Milton on his right forearm to high-five him. I am certain they are both making fun of me until Edith says, "Oh, leave the boys alone, Milton."

Gio laughs heartily. "It's no bother. Right, Rene?"

Gio shakes his head, so I do, too.

"Uh-oh," Milton grumbles. "Here comes the dog food . . ."

A nurse approaches us from behind, pushing a food cart. One of the wheels must be broken because the cart looks lopsided.

"So, darlings," she says, plastering a smile on her face, "eating inside or outside tonight?"

"Neither," Milton grumbles.

"Always a joker," she chuckles. She reaches into her cart and pulls out a beige tray with a clear plastic lid. "Mmmm, yummm."

Milton frowns at his meal: a block of chicken with yellow sauce, mashed potatoes, peas, a carton of white milk, and green Jell-O.

"Oh, it's not so bad," Edith says.

"You'll have to excuse Edith," Milton says. "She's losing her memory."

"Oh, Milton!"

"Well it must be true if you don't remember the taste of dog food." Milton gazes over my shoulder. "How perfect," he mutters. "Right on cue."

A small boy with a black soccer sweatshirt sprints past us. "I got these for you, grandpa," he calls, waving a Ziploc bag of cookies.

"Lucky bastard," Milton grunts.

"Milton! Watch your mouth around the boys," Edith says.

"Come on, Edith! They've heard worse. Hey, you fellas heard any good jokes? I'm old enough to handle dirty jokes, in case you got any dirty ones . . ."

Gio laughs. "Milton, you say that every time I come here."

"And you haven't learned yet! What kind of school do you go to anyway, where nobody tells any jokes? When are you boys gonna learn? Boy, if I didn't tell any jokes around here, I'd be dead . . . and I never would've met Edith."

Edith blushes. "It's true. We were sitting in the hallway reading a paper one day, and he told me a joke. I don't even remember it, but we've been together ever since."

"You don't *remember*?" Milton cries. "You really *are* losing your marbles!"

Edith rolls her eyes.

"It was like this," Milton says. "We were reading the newspaper and the nurse told us it was time for lunch, so I said, 'Hickory dickory dock, the mouse ran up the clock. The clock struck one . . . Lunch!' Then I stuck out my hand and said, 'Milton Hamsworth, pleased to meet you, beautiful.' And she swooned like a teenager after her first kiss. Oh, she swooned, baby."

"Oh, stop . . ."

"Anyway, boys," Milton says, rubbing the white stubble on his chin, "besides picking up chicks, jokes are like shooting stars or a lunar eclipse or this beautiful sunset. After a joke, you forget what you were upset about."

"That's why I come here," Gio says. "Clears my head." Then he turns to me and asks, "Does it work for you, too?"

I put a magnifying glass over my left eye, put on my archaeologist hat, peek inside my left brain, and notice that Johnny Van Slyke is nowhere to be seen.

ON MY WAY TO LUNCH THE NEXT DAY, I WALK WITH A BOP in my step, not as bouncy as Gio's step, but almost as bouncy because I am still basking in my glory. Not only did Milton hand me a bag of social tools, but Gio and I have something to talk about because we'll always have Milton and Edith. Anytime there's an awkward pause in our conversation, I can say, "So . . . Milton *really* doesn't like nursing home food, huh?" or "Edith is nicer than the lady we just met," or "Remember when we visited Milton and Edith?"

Plus, on the way home from the nursing home, Gio taught me a secret handshake which is great for obvious reasons. Things are going so well that I might find a few coins on the ground with their heads up. Or better yet, I might ask Ariel to sit with me during lunch. Maybe I'll even tell her a joke, not the one about the mouse running up a clock, but maybe another one.

Maybe it really *is* my lucky day: Ariel's red hair is twenty-four meters in front of me. I stick out my nose to inhale the red roses before they evaporate.

I wish Gio had walked me to lunch so that he could tell me how to talk or wave, or at least how to *look* at Ariel.

I really, really wish Gio had walked me to lunch when I feel a total of twelve teeth—six on the top, six on the bottom—chomping into my right shoulder. Since this isn't a movie and therefore it couldn't be Jaws or a radioactive spider, it has to be Johnny Van Slyke. And this is real, razor-sharp real, because Johnny's teeth are razor sharp, *way* sharper than they used to be. As his teeth sink deeper, deeper into my shoulder, I wonder if Johnny's dentist sharpened his teeth or if he recently became a vampire, but I can't tell if he's sucking my blood because the pain is razor sharp and paralyzing and I can't think of anything except hospitals and rabies and infectious diseases and—

"WHY ARE YOU BITING ME?" I scream out. I expect him to say, as he had before, that he didn't have time for lunch, but he says, "I'm biting you because you're a fruitcake with a big mouth. And, as you know, fruitcakes are food. So they must be bitten into." Up ahead, Ariel and her red roses disappear into the lunchroom.

His friend, Norman, cracks his knuckles and agrees with Johnny. Norman's hyena laugh is so fast and high-pitched that it pierces my skull, which could give me brain damage, and the more I think about brain damage, the more convinced I am that he really *is* giving me brain damage.

I can convince myself of anything. One time, in the fifth grade, I was stung by a bee. When the school nurse asked if I was allergic, I said that I wasn't (because I wasn't), but I convinced myself that I really *was* allergic, until my face felt as puffy as a marshmallow and my lungs overflowed with giant marshmallows until my throat swelled shut and I felt like I was going to fall to the floor and need those electronic thingies to rescue me as a circle of doctors and nurses yell, "CLEAR . . . One more time . . . CLEAR! Come on, damn you . . . CLEAR . . . He's gone. I'll tell his father. Oh, that's right, he doesn't have a father. I'll tell his mother."

Every time I see the footage of the Twin Towers crumbling on September 11, 2001, I convince myself that it's my fault, that I'm responsible. Though I was just a little kid when it happened, sometimes I blame myself because maybe I didn't go to church that day or shower correctly or complete all of my daily missions. Whenever I hear stories from grieving families or see pictures of firefighters in tears, I am so certain of my guilt that I can't sleep at night. I used to not sleep at all.

Anyway, as Norman is giving me brain damage, Johnny yanks me so close to his purple polo shirt that his right bicep pokes me in the eye. My body is a blanket of sweat. "LET ME GO YOU—" my new voice yells.

Johnny shoves me in the dirty bathroom. A windowless prison. Wet toilet paper stuck to broken tiles. Paper towels plugging cracks in the walls that look like ugly lightning bolts or tributaries from a filthy river. The stalls are dirty canvases, like art class for perverts: *For a good time, call Sharise . . . I already called her . . . The president is dumber than Sharise . . . Mr. Head is a dickhead.*

Johnny tugs me by the ear. "What should we do to him, Norman?"

Norman's hyena laugh gets louder, which makes my brain damage worse. Soon I will forget that Phil isn't a real father, that Ariel is an Angel, that Gio is my friend, that cereal is God's gift to mankind, that I can be courageous when I want to.

Gio, where *are* you?

"He *does* have a big mouth," Johnny says. "Maybe we should wash it out with soap, like his mommy should have done years ago."

Gio, Mr. Head—where *are* you guys?

Johnny pushes the metallic soap dispenser. Obviously, nothing comes out. Even *I* know there's never any soap in the bathroom—and I have brain damage.

The thought of swallowing soap flips my switch. I know I need to run, and in order to run, I need to be free.

I elbow Johnny in the stomach—hard. He releases me and clutches his stomach. Norman tries to grab me, but I duck under his arms and ram my recently bitten shoulder into the door. I cry in pain. It sounds like this: "Arrrrwwwwwwrrr-aaaaallllll!"

I sprint down the hall and smell my hand and glance at my Batman watch and notice that it's 12:28 and even with brain damage I know that 1 + 2 + 2 + 8 = 13 and I should've known I'd be attacked on a number thirteen and I think of waiting until 12:29 before taking another step but I don't have to wait any longer because suddenly I am in the air.

One of my classmates later told me that there were two Likegirls chatting in the middle of the hallway, and that I tried to dodge them at the last minute. All I remember is flying and then screaming, "Arrrrwwwwwwrrraaaaallllll!" and then cracking my head and seeing blackness with little white Christmas lights on top.

Johnny Van Slyke must be around here somewhere, up to his old tricks in Mr. Head's class, because the lights keep flicking on and then off.

On—and then off. On and then—off.

And then on.

"Rene, can you hear me? Rene, are you okay?"

That familiar voice again. It's Mr. Head. There are so many questions I have, and I don't know whether to ask them or not, but, as I've explained, my mom always says that I should, so I do.

"Mr. Head, did you know that Johnny attacked me for saving you during class?"

"I know, Rene, but please relax."

"Does Gio know that Johnny attacked me for saving you during class?"

"He'll be here soon. Take it easy, okay?"

"You know Johnny attacked me, right?"

"Yes, I do." He takes a deep breath. "Rene, you shouldn't have stuck up for me and you shouldn't have blown up in class. And you should never curse in class, *ever*, especially at someone like Johnny, because—"

"Did Ariel see me fall?"

"Who?"

"You know, Ariel."

"Who's Ariel?"

"The Angel of Angels."

"Breathe deeply and try not to move."

"Don't tell her I said that, though, okay?"

"Said what?"

"That she's the Angel of Angels. She doesn't know. If she knew, she wouldn't be the Angel of Angels anymore."

"Please, Rene, breathe through your nose."

"I am. And I don't smell red roses, so I know she isn't here."

"Please stop talking, Rene."

"Do you know that I have brain damage?"

He pauses. I think he's wondering if I've always had brain damage, and if that's the reason I slept on his desk.

"Are you still leaving the school?" I ask.

"Relax, Rene. Everything will be fine."

I know he's lying because "Everything will be fine" is a secret code for "Things will become much more difficult in the very near future."

And then I sort of start crying. I mean, not like a crocodile or a waterfall or anything, but my eyes are damp, and the more I try to wipe the dampness away, the damper they get. Mr. Head must have seen the dampness in my eyes, because he says, "Don't worry. I've already called your home."

I don't want to admit to him that this makes me happy because my mom *does* make me feel better when I'm upset, even when, like today, I'm still mad at her, but I want to know what "soon" means and don't want Mr. Head to think I'm ignoring him, so I say, "When is my mom coming?"

"Your mom had to go to work," he says, "so she won't be able to pick you up."

I try to explain to Mr. Head that it's not possible and that he must be confused, but I understand what he means and I understand what day it is. Doomsday. My nightmare has come true: not the one about a milkman delivering milk to my house, the one in which the milkman says, "Good afternoon, here is your milk . . ." Then he rotates the milk carton and points at a picture of a missing boy. It's a picture of me. The milkman grabs me by the hair and throws me into the backseat of his milkmobile.

No, this nightmare is far worse than the milkman nightmare, because it's real—and far more frightening. A ghost is crawling out of a grave and knocking on my door. Ghosts belong in scary scenes in scary movies, not at Radcliffe High School.

"Is it a man?" I ask.

Please no.

"Yes."

"Is he coming to school?"

Please no.

"Yes."

"Is he coming right now?"

Please no.

"Yes."

"His name . . ."

Please no. Please no. Please.

"Phil."

Silence.

"Is Phil your dad?"

"No."

"Well, he's the one I spoke to. He seemed really nice, too. And considerate. And funny. I really enjoyed our conversation."

"How—how did you reach him?"

"I already told you, Rene. I called your house."

I take three deep breaths and *then* think. I think Phil is tired of mailing me $2 bills and a note about not being a monster. I think Phil is at my house. I think he is there with my mom. I think my mom wants me to see Phil.

Phil, who I haven't seen in six years, who I hate more than I hate the principal taking credit for all the stupid trophies other kids earned, more than I hate Johnny Van Slyke when he's a rattlesnake . . . Phil, my ex-dad, is coming to school.

What did I do wrong? Did I step on too many cracks? Collect the wrong rubber bands? Pick up an unlucky coin? Not wash my hands? Not tap my locker? Not smell my hands? Did I wake up on a number thirteen? Was it 7:06? 7:15? 7:33? 8:32?

I wish I could turn off the lights, all the lights in this hallway, at this school, in my neighborhood, in my street, and in my head. But it's bright inside, and it's bright *outside,* where the sun is shining and Phil must be getting into his car, strapping on his seat belt, putting the car in drive, and stepping on the gas in order to see me, his ex-son.

I am six years old. I am waiting outside my school. The sky is purple and pink. I am wearing green gloves and a red scarf. Both the gloves and the scarf are wet with white snot. I can't stop sneezing. Phil is supposed to pick me up but he's not here. My teacher, Mrs. Wellington, keeps looking at her Mickey Mouse watch. Mrs. Wellington doesn't have gloves or a scarf. Her nose is as red as Rudolph the red-nosed reindeer's. I want to laugh, because picturing Mrs. Wellington pulling Santa Claus in a sleigh is funny, but I keep sneezing. She tells me to cover my mouth. She is standing far away from me so that I don't sneeze on her.

"Are you sure *your dad knows he's supposed to pick you up?" she asks.*

"Yes," I say, but she doesn't believe me. She hands me her cell phone. I know my phone number by heart. I call, but nobody answers.

The sky is getting dark.

She checks her watch again. I ask if I can inspect it. She says okay. Mickey Mouse is smiling. His right hand is on the number 7.

Her eyes go back and forth between her watch and the sky. I think she is praying, or at least praying on the inside like I do.

"Excuse me, Rene," she says, "but I need to make a few phone calls. I was supposed to be home two hours ago. I have kids of my own, you know."

She takes eight steps to the side and puts the phone to her ear.

There are only four stars in the sky, which isn't a lot. I sit on a bench and play myself in thumb war. My left hand wins. I play again. My right hand wins this time, but it doesn't really *win because it cheated: my right index finger did a sneak attack on my left thumb.*

"I know . . ." Mrs. Wellington mumbles. "As soon as I can . . ."

Although it's dark outside, I can still see colors, bright colors, on the front entrance of the school, where the art teacher hangs "stellar student work." My art isn't stellar, so it's not there. I whisper to myself, "I spy with my little eye the color blue." I beat myself in this game because I already know what I'm spying on . . . after all, it's my *little eye. I change the rules. I tell myself, "I spy with my little right eye the color green." I close my right eye and look around for green things with my left eye. The game is still too easy so I play a new one.*

I try to walk around the bench without touching any of the cracks in the concrete with my feet. Some kids at school say that if you step on a crack, you'll break your mother's back, but I don't like these rules because it's hard to sleep at night when at any second my mother's back could break—and I'd have to rush her to the hospital and tell the doctors and Phil that I'm the one to blame for my mom never walking again.

I change the rules to make it less scary. If I step on a crack, Phil won't come to pick me up, which isn't scary because I don't even want *him to pick me up. On my fourth step, my left toe touches a crack. Oh, well. Since Phil isn't ever going to pick me up, I lie down on the bench.*

"Yeah, I'm still here," Mrs. Wellington says over the phone. "Some nerve."

I close my eyes and hope a police officer or a firefighter or a superhero comes to rescue me before a robber either robs or kidnaps me. The more I think about robbers, the more I sweat. Before long, I am sweating a lot, even on my nose. I take off my sweaty, snotty green gloves and red scarf and put them on the ground. Even though the ground is dirty, I would rather have them there, because I don't like snotty, sweaty things next to me.

I close my eyes again. I hear a car coming. Or is it a truck? A fire truck? I keep my eyes closed and pray. Please let it be a firefighter in a fire truck. Please let it be a firefighter in a fire truck. The vehicle is coming closer.

I know it's not a firefighter in a fire truck when I hear, "Yo, Rene, what the hell are you lying on that dirty bench for?"

It's Phil. Although I tell myself not to, I stand up and walk to the car.

"About time," Mrs. Wellington mutters.

"Yo, Rene!" Phil shouts. "Are you just gonna leave *your new gloves and scarf?"*

I walk back to the bench.

"Good night, Rene," Mrs. Wellington calls, hustling to her car.

I wave.

"Good night, teacher," Phil grunts. Then he turns to me. "Why the hell did you put your new gloves and scarf on the dirty ground?"

I pick up my things and walk back to the car.

"Gotta be more responsible, Rene. Gotta use your head."

Phil keeps wiping his nose, even though he doesn't have any boogers or blood coming out. He smells like cigarettes. His hands are shaking against the steering wheel.

I AM SIX AND ONE HALF YEARS OLD. PHIL IS WRITING A story on the inside of his green notebook. His handwriting is fancy and slanted. It's 8:57, twenty-seven minutes past my bedtime, but I want to watch Phil write.

He has been writing for the past forty-six minutes, has downed six cups of coffee. His eyes dance back and forth from his notebook to tiny scraps of paper—napkins, receipts, business cards—on which he has written notes for his stories. He wiggles his tongue from side to side as he ponders his next sentence.

Phil hates it when I talk to him or stand next to him while he's writing, but I really want to know what he's writing about. I tell myself not to, but I tiptoe behind him and peek over his shoulder. He smells like leather mixed with oranges.

On one of the napkins is the word "theft"; on another

napkin is the word "clarity"; there are two words on the back of a receipt: "family reunion." Phil has told me that he, like me, is good at word association, and that he can write a whole story simply by remembering one or two words. There's a word written in red ink on a scrap of newspaper, but I can't read it because it's too small. I lean in closer.

"God damn it, Rene, you know I hate it, really hate it, when you look over my shoulder."

"But I want to see what you're writing."

"Well, when I finally get published, I'll let you read my stories."

"Is that a deal?" I ask, because deals are inside jokes that involve two people and I want my dad and me to share a lot of inside jokes.

"Whatever," he says, and goes back to writing his story.

I AM SIX AND SEVEN-TWELFTHS YEARS OLD. I AM EATING A Fruit Roll-Up for breakfast even though I know Fruit Roll-Ups should only be eaten after lunch. Phil is wearing an old baseball T-shirt and blue jeans. His teeth are clenched. He is banging his fist on his green notebook.

When my mom asks him what is wrong, he says, "Honey, last night, my writing sparkled like gold, the kind of gold you could buy with a good night at the slots, or at craps, or at roulette. But in the morning, in the light of day, I can see that what I wrote was fool's gold."

My mom goes back to doing laundry. Phil goes into his room and closes his door and watches television. I put my ear against his door. He is watching The Price Is Right. *He is punching the wall.*

I AM SEVEN YEARS OLD TODAY. PHIL DIDN'T WANT TO GO TO Wendy's like we always do on my birthday, so we are at Chili's. My mom invited a few of her work friends, and they brought along their kids.

Our waitress walks over to our table:

Phil: "Psst, yo, Rene."

[Phil kicks me in the right shin.]

Me: "What gives?"

Phil: "Hottie at six o'clock."

Waitress: "Good evening, my name is Ariel. I'll be your server this evening."

Phil: "Good evening, Ariel, you're as beautiful as a mermaid."

Waitress: "Um . . . thanks?"

Phil: "You know, like Ariel from The Little Mermaid*... Rene here used to sing that "seaweed-is-always-greener" song and everybody laughed at him because—"*

Mom: "That's enough, Phil! You're embarrassing him! Look, he's blushing."

Phil: "Well, Ariel, since you already introduced yourself, *let me introduce you to my beautiful family. I'm Phil, and this here is my son, Rene, whose face, as you can see, is red like your lobster friend—what's his name again?"*

Me: "His name is Sebastian, but she's not really Ar—"

Phil: "Hah! I knew you'd remember. Anyway, Ariel, I'm Phil, this is Rene, and this is my wife, Susan, and her friends. Susan here thought it would be a good idea not to embarrass Rene on his birthday—you know, with him not having any friends and all—so Susan told her friends to bring their kids so it would look like Rene's a normal kid celebrating his birthday with all his closest friends and family."

I AM SEVEN AND THREE-QUARTERS YEARS OLD. I AM WEARING my good-luck soccer sweatshirt. Phil, my mom, and I are eating pizza at Joe's Pizza on a Sunday night. Eating at a restaurant is a special thing because I'm allowed to drink soda there. I order Mountain Dew, even though Johnny Van Slyke tells everyone at school that Mountain Dew lowers your sperm count—whatever that *means. Phil is drinking his fourth beer.*

The bright red sign for Joe's Pizza is missing a Z. A man peers in the window; his face is where the Z should be. He has blue eyes. The man is homeless; I've seen him sleeping on the sidewalk outside the restaurant. It's 24 degrees Fahrenheit outside but the man isn't wearing a hat or gloves. He has a big gray blanket wrapped around him.

We order mushroom pizza because Phil likes mushrooms. I eat two slices and then get full because I refilled my soda four times. There are two extra slices. I grab a napkin and tear at its edges until I have three small pieces and one big piece. I roll the three small pieces into tiny balls and curve the one larger piece into a horseshoe. I put them on the table and align my smiley face.

Phil doesn't talk during our meal. He stares through my mom and me as if we're invisible. Every few minutes, he writes notes to himself on napkins or receipts or ticket stubs with his blue pen, but he doesn't say a word. When he's like that, I don't say anything either because I don't like talking when it's too quiet. I hate when Phil doesn't talk to me because it makes me feel like he doesn't like me, which makes me *not like me. The quieter it is, the more I don't like myself.*

The whole meal passes in silence. It feels like a funeral, and funerals, even imaginary ones, make me sad.

Phil waves at the waiter and asks for the check. The waiter asks me if I want to take the last two slices home. I say that I do, not because I'm hungry but because while Phil was staring over my shoulder, I was staring over his at the homeless guy with blue eyes and the big gray blanket.

My mom tells me that giving something to someone in need is a cure for feeling lousy. It sounds crazy, but she's right. Sometimes I give my Cheetos to classmates during lunch and it makes me feel like a million dollars.

I don't have a million dollars to give the homeless man, but I do have a bag with two slices of mushroom pizza in it. When we leave the restaurant, on the way to our car, I hand the bag to the homeless man. I feel great about myself until Phil makes a loud noise. At first, I think he yells "Hot!" as in "The pizza is hot, *don't burn yourself," but he isn't yelling "hot."*

He is laughing.

I AM SEVEN AND FIVE-SIXTHS YEARS OLD. PHIL, MY MOM, and I arrive at the beach in Atlantic City. We take our sandals off because the sand is made for your feet like peanut butter is made for jelly. But today the sand is hot, like flaming coals on a barbecue, so my mom and I run to a spot and throw the blanket down and step on it so our feet don't burn off.

Phil walks slowly to the blanket. He didn't want to wake up this morning and he didn't want to come to the beach because the casinos had "ripped his heart out and stolen his soul"—whatever that *means.*

I take off my blue T-shirt with a soccer ball on it and immediately cover myself with sunblock so the sun can't cook me for lunch. Phil takes off his Caesar's Palace shirt. He is an orangutan with red and orange hair all over his chest and back.

I cover my mouth so that I don't giggle. My mom walks over to me and whispers in my ear to tell Phil to take his shirt off. Since she knows everything, she knows that I don't understand her joke. She explains it to me so that I understand. It is an inside joke, and I am happy to be on the inside.

I turn to Phil. "You should take your shirt off because it's really hot outside."

He doesn't laugh.

I glance at my mom. She shrugs her shoulders.

I want Phil to laugh so I tell my own inside joke. "Look, Daddy, it's a monster," I say, pointing at him.

He doesn't laugh.

I AM EIGHT YEARS OLD. I AM EATING A BAGEL WITH CREAM cheese and grape jelly. My mom is wearing a red sweater with a dog on it. It is 2:55 p.m. There are three poker chips on the floor. They are facedown, so I don't pick them up.

My mom's hair is light brown. It smells like flowers. She is ironing my white shirt with white buttons. She keeps pressing the same spot, the right sleeve, over and over again, even though it's already perfect and smooth.

Phil's green notebook is on the kitchen table.

I ask my mom if Phil is a good writer. She says, "Your father is an excellent writer."

"Then why hasn't he written any books?"

"Because . . . because you can't control what other people think."

I want to tell her that I can't even control what I *think, but I don't want to upset her. She's already upset at Phil, but she won't tell me why. She never tells me why, because she doesn't like to talk about big things. So instead of asking "Does Dad love me?" or "Does he think of me when he writes?" I just ask, "Where's Dad?"*

She stops ironing the right shoulder of my white shirt with white buttons. She takes a deep breath, a very deep breath, and says, "Rene, I don't know how to say this, so I'm just going to say it."

She takes another deep breath. It's 2:56 p.m. Her perfume smells like roses. "Rene, your father isn't coming back."

My mom is a liar.

Phil *is* coming back. I don't want to see him and I don't want him to see me, especially while I'm lying on the dirty floor with a leaking bag of ice dripping on my swollen head.

I shift my body to get up but the room spins like a ballerina in a white dress.

Mr. Head steadies me. "Whoa there, Rene, I told you to take it easy."

"But Phil—"

"Your dad."

"Kind of," I protest.

"I don't understand."

"Forget it. I need to go to the boys' bathroom."

"Well, maybe Gio can help you when he gets here," Mr. Head tells me. "He's on his way."

Since I don't want Gio to see me like this either, I stand up even though the room is tilting from side to side. I want to get to the bathroom but I'm walking sideways; I bump into a locker that isn't mine. I push myself off and walk diagonally in the other direction.

I think I'm going to bump into another locker when Mr. Head says, "Here, let me help you." He lifts my arm over his shoulder and guides me in a straight line. This is what friends do for each other when one of them is dizzy but needs to use the bathroom.

"There," he says, opening the door to the boys' bathroom. "I'll wait outside."

I walk to the mirror. Even though it isn't foggy, I can't see myself clearly. I splash water on my face. It feels refreshing, but it doesn't make me look any clearer.

I can hear Phil's voice outside the boys' bathroom. I know it's not a daydream because Mr. Head is answering Phil. I hear the word "head," but I don't know if Mr. Head is telling Phil that I bumped my *head* because I'm a dirty, stupid moron who tripped over two Likegirls while running away from Johnny Van Slyke, or if Mr. Head is introducing himself, as in "Hello, my name is Mr. *Head,* the teacher whose room your ex-son slept in the night before last." I don't know which is worse, and I don't want to hear any more, so I walk into a stall and lock the door and sit on the toilet with all my clothes on.

I smell my left hand. It smells like a #2, even though I haven't gone #2, and thinking of #2's makes me laugh because I love bathroom humor. I loved bathroom humor before Milton told me the power of jokes. Bathroom humor is the best kind of humor because unlike wry, sarcastic, and inside-joke humor, people of every age can appreciate it. Especially in times like these. Since I want to make time stand still and become invisible, I try to list each of the names associated with a #2: butt, bottom, ass, a booty, bum, poop, shit, crap, feces, turds, dump, caca, rocks, pebbles, doo-doo, dropping anchor, baking brownies. This makes me feel better so I tell myself my favorite joke: Why do policemen smell? Because they're always on duty.

Even though I didn't go #2, I convince myself that I did, and since I wiped my butt/bottom/ass/booty/bum, there must still be some microscopic poop/shit/crap/feces/turds/brownies/caca/rocks/pebbles/doo-doo on my right hand, so if I had my pants down, I would pick them up and button my button and zip up my zipper with my *left* hand, then unlatch the door with my left hand, which I do now. If there was soap in the soap dispenser, which obviously there isn't or else Johnny Van Slyke would have shoved it in my mouth, I would put some soap in my left hand, but since there obviously *isn't* any soap, I wet my hands which helps eliminate *some* but not *all* of the poop/shit/crap/feces/turds/brownies/caca/rocks/pebbles/doo-doo on my right hand, so I turn on the faucet with my left hand so that my right hand, which has microscopic poop/shit/crap/feces/turds/brownies/caca/rocks/pebbles/doo-doo on it, doesn't put the microscopic dirty stuff on the faucet for everyone else to touch.

If you were wondering why I only smell my *left* hand when I'm nervous, now you know.

"HIGH-FIVE, CHAMP," PHIL SAYS AS I WALK OUT OF THE bathroom.

I don't know if he wants to give me a high five because I finally got out of the bathroom or because he thinks that my tripping over two Likegirls is funny; that my trying to save Mr. Head is heroic; or because he hasn't seen me in six years and doesn't know whether I want to hug or kiss him.

I don't.

I don't want to hug him *or* kiss him or even high-five him, but since Mr. Head is standing next to Phil, and I don't want Mr. Head to get any more upset and therefore want to quit even sooner than he already wants to, I give Phil a high five, but not a hard high five like you would if someone trapped a thousand fireflies in a jar or won a million dollars in the lottery or banged a rock with a hammer and found hundreds of sparkling white and pink crystals.

"Ready to go, champ?" he asks.

I'm not ready to go, but if I don't go, Gio will see how scared I am of Phil and of falling down and busting my head, so he'll worry about me and maybe even not sleep tonight because he is so worried; and if he doesn't sleep, he will be super-tired when he comes to school tomorrow, which means that he'll be unable to focus and will want to cut classes, which will make Mr. Head mad at him and mad at himself and therefore want to quit on us; and the principal will blame me and eventually trace the evidence back to me because I did, after all, sleep on Mr. Head's desk and rummage through his private stuff, which means that my fingerprints are sprawled all over the crime scene . . . so I say, "Yes. Let's go home."

"THIS WAY, CHAMP," HE SAYS, AS WE WALK TOWARD THE parking lot.

If I were a champ, I would know how to fight. If I knew how to fight, I would fight Phil, right here, right now, bare-knuckled and bloody. I wouldn't mind the blood; his blood is my blood. I would knock him down with my right fist, pin his arms down with my knees, and rail on him for all the years he left me wondering where he went, why he didn't take me, why I split up my parents, why I made my mom miserable, why I don't have a father.

If I were a champ, I'd reach into my wallet and pull out a few $2 bills, stuff them in his mouth, and say, "You *are* a monster."

If I were a champ, I would rain my punches on him for each of the promises he broke; for everything that I wanted him to be; for everything that he isn't; and for everything that I am not.

"Third car on the right, champ," Phil says. I count: a tall black truck, a navy blue Cadillac, and then a small, red car.

And then I get this feeling, like a suddenly suspicious and clear-minded actor does in a scary scene in a scary movie, that I have been here before. I have seen this red car. Not in my daydreams or in my childhood. No, I have been here recently, seen this car recently, as recently as . . .

It's on the tip of my brain as I strap on my seat belt and look over at Phil. He doesn't have much hair left. The hair that he *does* have is shaped like an upside down T. I stare out the window and try not to blink . . .

Blink! That's it: I was leaning my sweaty forehead on the windowpane in my room, trying not to blink. That's when I saw it. The small red car . . . a balding, snoring man . . . ordered to sleep in the car by his wife . . . she had a big day ahead of her, this woman . . . my mom! Phil slept near me! Across the street! He's been . . . to my house! She—my mom didn't tell me!

"You all right, champ?" Phil asks.

I talk about small things because I don't want to talk about any big things like why Phil slept outside my house, why Phil is *here*, why Phil is here *now*, and why Phil is here now with *me* in his small, red car.

"It's sunny outside," I say.

"Yes it is, champ. Beautiful day for a drive, even if it is a quick one."

He means we are almost done driving, which means that we are going to my house. He isn't asking for directions.

It's getting harder and harder to breathe, so I focus my eyes on something else. Phil is wearing a polo shirt with a small bird on the top left-hand side, which I like because I like nature, especially birds, because when Phil used to take me to the zoo . . . Well, remember how I told you that I was afraid of orangutans because I thought they were monsters? The only animals that I *wasn't* afraid of were the pigeons. I used to chase after them, bobbing my head and flashing my claws, yelling "Rarrrrrr" so they would be scared of me and fly away. They probably thought that I wanted to catch them and tear their heads off or something. I did. I mean, I wanted to catch them, not tear their heads off. I wasn't strong enough to do that.

Phil must have seen me looking at the small bird on the top left-hand side of his shirt because as we pull up to *my* house, he says in his friendliest tone, "Still like animals, huh? Remember how I got you that subscription for *National Geographic* cards?"

For a few years, I got *National Geographic* cards in the mail. Instead of baseball cards, I got a gorilla card or a zebra card or an armadillo card with a few cool facts about them on the back. I threw them out when Phil left. I mean, I drew on them with permanent black marker and then ripped them into tiny little pieces and stepped on them and spat on them and *then* threw them out.

We pull into the driveway. *My* driveway. Phil smells like leather mixed with oranges. I know it would be polite to ask how his writing is going but I need to leave the car NOW! NOW! NOW! My bones are busting out of my skin, so I open the car door and hear *ding . . . ding . . . ding . . .*

"Rene, I want to talk with you." Phil unbuckles his seat belt.

"I don't want to talk with you!" I shout, sprinting to the front door. I let myself in and shut the door—*my* door—and lock it and tell Phil to stay away, and then I plan out in my head how I am going to save Mr. Head from quitting and how Ariel and I will get married in a garden of red roses and how Gio will become my best man; and since it's all too much to keep track of, I run into my room and put on my Batman cape and crawl into a ball, which reminds me of sleeping on Mr. Head's desk, so I take it off and I don't want to see it anymore because then I'll think about it and I'll think about it and I'll think about it, so I throw it in the back corner of my closet and I close my eyes and sit, Indian style, on the red carpet floor and tell myself jokes, like, Why do policemen always smell?

I AM ELEVEN AND A HALF YEARS OLD. IT'S DARK OUTSIDE but plenty bright inside room 132. It's father-son night at school. Phil has been gone for three years, so my mom is sitting next to me.

Mr. Walsh, my sixth-grade teacher, is at the front of the room pointing to a plastic penis. "This here is the penis—the tree, if you will—and all around the penis is pubic hair—or the forest—which, young men, you will start seeing pretty soon—if you haven't seen it already."

I tell my mom that I need to go to the bathroom. She says, "It's locked." I tell her that I need a drink at the water fountain. She says, "It's broken." I tell her that I need air. She says, "The window is open. It's freezing in here."

She pats the chair, which means that I should sit back down.

"This here is a condom," says Mr. Walsh. "Very important. Here, let me open it. Hold on . . . this'll only take a sec . . . gotta tear this dang wrapper . . . maybe tear it from the top . . . okay, now we're in business . . . you open it up . . . from the other side . . . and fit it over . . ."

My mom is trying not to laugh. She isn't trying hard

enough. I wish she would stop. Not only is she the only woman there, she's the only one of thirty—no, wait, thirty-two—people in the room laughing.

"Where's Phil?" I ask so that she'll stop laughing, and because for the first time in a long time, I actually want him around.

"Pay attention to Mr. Walsh, sweetie," she says.

"Listen up, men," Mr. Walsh says. "That's right, you're becoming men, and as men, you'll have nights when you wake up to find your sheets sticky and wet with a gelatinous white goo. Your first thought will be, 'Oh, Lord, I peed my pants.' Now, don't be frightened. No, no, it's perfectly normal. It's only your sperm . . . er . . . recycling *itself . . . er . . . like we recycle paper at school. But sperm is more . . . er . . . important and powerful than paper because sperm is what we need in order to make a baby with a woman. And with power comes responsibility."*

I AM ELEVEN AND SEVEN-TWELFTHS YEARS OLD. THERE'S A beautiful woman with me at the beach. No, she is a mermaid. She has a long green fin and red hair. Seagulls are singing. The sun is setting. The mermaid takes off her bra. Her breasts are the size of volleyballs. She asks me to touch her. I do.

I open my eyes. I'm sweating. No, it can't be sweat; there's too much liquid. It must be pee. There's pee on my red Superman sheets. I don't know how to tell my mom that I peed in my pants. I think I'll tell her I got scared after watching a scary scene in a scary movie—no, that I drank too much Mountain Dew. Way too much Mountain Dew. They had free refills at lunch.

Then I remember Mr. Walsh and what Johnny Van Slyke told me about Mountain Dew. I think Mr. Walsh is right and that Johnny Van Slyke is wrong. Mountain Dew definitely *does not lower your sperm count.*

Now I'm really sweating, I mean really *sweating, because the sperm in my bed can actually make a woman pregnant and have a baby, and the only woman in the house is my mom and, with Phil gone, I definitely don't want* her *to touch the sperm and get pregnant and have another baby.*

"With power comes responsibility," Mr. Walsh had said. I know what I must do. I must destroy the sperm.

I wrap up my red Superman sheets, being sure not to touch the powerful sperm that could make my mom pregnant. But my right index finger gets wet. I wipe it on my Superman sheets and crumble the sheets into a ball and tiptoe to the front door. I open the door and creep down the driveway. I can see my breath. The concrete is cold against my bare feet. I stuff the sheets into a steel garbage can and shut the lid.

Done. Destroyed. I think my family is safe until I realize that my underwear is still wet and that my right index finger, which had come in contact with the powerful sperm, had touched the doorknob on the front door and *the lid of the garbage can. Since I don't want my mom to touch these objects and therefore get pregnant, I spend the rest of the night cleaning the doorknob and the garbage can lid and my hands, scrubbing and scrubbing with detergent until the sun rises and my fingers are red and raw but my family is safe and I declare myself a superhero.*

I OPEN MY EYES. IT IS MORNING. I AM IN MY ROOM, AS always. My room is clean, as always. I have sand in my eyes, as always. But something is wrong. Something is terribly wrong.

The lights are on . . . I'm lying on my red carpet . . . wearing all my clothes . . . I feel sweaty . . . *oh, no, please no* . . . My underwear feels wet . . . *oh, no, please no* . . . I hold my breath . . . *please, please* . . .

Thank you, God, I'm only sweating. I exhale. Wait, why am I sweating? I have all my clothes on. No, there's something else, someone else. Gio? Still my friend. Ariel? Still unmarried. Mr. Head? Still at school. Mom? Still alive. Phil? Still . . . here?

He . . . picked me up at school . . . gave me a high five . . . met Mr. Head . . . called me "champ" . . . I didn't punch him . . . We got into his small, red car . . . He had a shirt with a bird on it . . . He smelled like leather and oranges . . . I ran in here . . . He . . .

I pick myself off the carpet and try not to blink, but my eyes aren't listening, so I close them. My forehead is sweating buckets. I run to the window and rest my face on the cold windowpane.

With my eyes still closed, I paint a picture in my head of a quiet, empty street with no red cars. Birds chirp at one another, exchanging pleasantries. A red bird tells a blue bird that it will be a marvelous day with nothing to be scared of. The blue bird agrees. Below them, caterpillars crawl on the cold, quiet sidewalk. They have nowhere to be, nothing to worry about, no parents coming back from the grave. Ariel scoops a caterpillar into her hands. She waves at me and smiles. And even though it's daytime, fireflies wink their bright tails, signaling that it's okay for me to open my eyes.

I crack open my right eye. Phil's red car is parked on the street. Phil isn't sleeping in it.

Why did the cookie go to the nurse's office? Because he was feeling crummy. Why did the turtle cross the road? To get to the shell station. Why do policemen always smell? Because they're always on duty. A horse walks into a bar; the bartender says, "Why the long—?"

There's a knock at my door, then three more knocks, which is a secret code for my mom. "Honey, come on out."

I don't feel like honey. I feel like paint: slow, smelly, and poisonous.

"We really need to talk, honey," she says. "I know you're upset, but this is all a big misunderstanding. Come on out so that we can talk about it."

"I don't want to talk!"

"There's breakfast on the table . . ."

"I'm not hungry," I lie.

"Rene, if you don't come out, you'll be late for school."

Even though I am firecracker mad at my mom for bringing Phil back and not telling me, it's not my mission to make her late today. No, today's mission is to ask Gio what to do about Phil. I unlock my door and walk to the kitchen for breakfast.

And lose my appetite immediately.

Phil, in his large white underwear, with his large stomach drooping over the elastic strip, is flipping pancakes. His hairy chest and hairy back and hairy stomach and hairy legs and hairy feet have gotten hairier.

The sizzling batter is bubbling. It smells like burnt butter.

Phil, with all his red chest and back and stomach hair, is standing over the griddle, manning my breakfast, and I don't know what scares me the most: Phil being in my house, Phil being in his underwear, or Phil's hairs falling in the pancake batter and blending into my pancakes and then burying themselves in my stomach until I choke on them and Mr. Head has to give me the Heimlich maneuver, which won't work because he doesn't know the Heimlich maneuver so the nurse will have to rush me to the hospital in a screaming ambulance until the doctor reaches down my throat and says, "There we go, kiddo, all better. You swallowed a hair, probably belonging to a large man, most likely from the large man's back, and this large man, as confirmed by DNA testing, is your father."

"Good morning, champ," Phil says, licking pancake batter off his fingers.

My mom takes a deep breath. "This is not what it seems. Honey, I'd like for us all to talk for a few minutes before you leave for school."

"But—I—I need to leave now." I scramble for my bookbag.

"Don't forget your breakfast!" Phil hollers, but I'm already out the door.

THE CHEESE BUS—THAT'S WHAT EVERYONE AT SCHOOL CALLS the yellow school bus—arrives at the corner of Frankfurt Street and Second Avenue every morning at 7:22 sharp, except this morning. It arrives at 7:24, which is a bad luck time because $7+2+4=13$. I need better luck at school than I had at home, so as the bus pulls up to the corner, I unzip my backpack and dump it upside down. Everything falls out.

"Oh, *man*!" I yell, so that Ms. Donna, the bus driver, can hear me and doesn't think I dropped everything on purpose.

The bus hums in place as Ms. Donna, whose voice sounds like an old door creaking shut in a scary scene in a scary movie, shouts, "Hurry up, will ya?"

I put my knees on the dirty ground and pick up four sharp #2 pencils, two dull #2 pencils, two pink erasers, three empty notebooks, two textbooks, and a black-and-white composition book for English class.

It's now 7:25, and $7+2+5=14$, not 13. I climb three steps and sit in the front row right behind Ms. Donna, who is hollering at kids to "quit agitating back there" and "sit ya butts in the seat or I'll *glue* ya butts to the seat."

I sit my butt in a seat big enough for two butts. There are no other butts in the seat because I like to sit alone.

I'm behind in my journal entries because of Phil's arrival and my busted head. I need to write all three journal entries this morning. I change the dates of the last two entries so that Mr. Head thinks I actually read those books. Even though I hate lying to Mr. Head, this is Mr. Head's big week. He needs me to save him:

September 27

Good morning, my good friend. I hope you slept well last night and that you didn't sleep on your cold and lonely desk. I would know. LOL. Anyway, last night I read pages 35–55 in a book about how one teacher in Los Angeles rescued her students by convincing them to write in their journals. I used the reading strategy of connecting because she reminded me of you.

September 28

Hello, my fellow friend. I hope this finds you alive and well at Radcliffe High School. Last night, I read pages 60–78 in a book about crime fighting. There were two men trying to eliminate crime in the city of Gotham. I used the reading strategy of connecting because we stopped Johnny Van Slyke and his cronies from committing crimes in your room. You are the hero; I am merely your loyal sidekick.

September 29

Greetings, heroic friend of mine. On the bus ride to school this morning, I read pages 20–34 in a book about a scarlet pimple—I think it's a Scarlet Pimpernel, but I picture him as a pimple—stealing from the rich and giving to the poor. Since you are a teacher, and are therefore poor, I thought of you. I visualize you riding into town on a big brown horse throwing gold nuggets of knowledge to hordes of screaming, happy children. I am the screaming, happy child in the back, gnawing on a turkey leg while stuffing gold in my brain.

"So are you gonna leave or are you just gonna sit with your butt glued to that seat?" Ms. Donna wants to know.

I'm the only one left on the bus. I don't want to get trapped, so I pack up my reading journal, thank Ms. Donna for driving safely, and step off the bus.

I follow the crowd through the heavy doors into the school. Not that I have a choice.

Gio is waiting by the trophy case, which makes me feel like gold. His goatee grew overnight. It reminds me of a goat. I am allergic to goats but not to Gio. Even if I were allergic to Gio, I would still go near him because we are friends, best friends, and—

"I heard what happened," he says.

"About—"

"Mr. Head and I had a long talk, a good talk, an adult talk, about his journal and Johnny Van Slyke. As you know, I think what you did for Mr. Head was great."

I smile. "B'noodles, right?"

Two Devilblackcoats walk past me. Their devil rings look scary, but I'm not scared because Gio is next to me.

"It was definitely b'noodles. But Mr. Head spoke to me about how what *I've* been doing isn't b'noodles. You know, with the cutting. But he told me that I was one of the people he doesn't worry about because I've got my head on my shoulders." He pauses. "He knows I'm mature and that I'll eventually figure things out but—"

I know what he means so I cut him off. "But he worries about me because I *won't* figure things out, because I *don't* have my head on my shoulders."

"Well, not exactly, Rene."

"Is this because of Phil?"

"You mean, your dad," he says.

"He used to be my dad," I explain. "But he's back. That's why I ran away from home this morning."

Gio's eyes go big. "You ran away from *home*?"

"Yes, I ran to the bus earlier than usual. From home."

"Oh, Jesus H. Christ. You scared me."

"Jesus *H.* Christ?"

"Yeah, *H,*" Gio says. "You know, for Harry. His middle name."

Even though I have a lot on my mind, I laugh because I can't believe that every Sunday I pray to a guy named Harry, which sounds almost as boring as the name of my dad's hero, Robert Zimmerman.

Anyway, we are running out of time because the bell is about to ring so I say, "Anyway, we are running out of time because the bell is about to ring."

"Look, brother man," he says. "The bell is only a suggestion, or, um, *recommendation,* to go to class. It's like someone saying, 'Here's some ketchup, I *recommend* it on your fries.' It's not like an emergency siren for an earthquake or an ambulance, you know?"

"No."

"Look, sometimes you gotta live your life like you only got one. Breathe like you only got a few breaths left. Be spontaneous, brother man, instead of thinking every decision through like the whole world hangs in the balance."

I know that he is wrong, so I reach for weapons of guilt. "But Mr. Head told you not to cut."

"Sure, we spoke—I mean, he spoke to me—but I need to live my life just like he needs to live his. Right now, he's not living his. That's why he wants to steal my line and tell the students and principal to get off his biscuit."

"But Milton told you to take better notes. How can you take better notes if—"

"Look," Gio says. "We *do* need to help Mr. Head. And I *will* go to his class. And, of course, I'll go to Mr. Chalmers's class. But I'm tired of everyone thinking they know what's best for me; that they know me better than I know myself; that they can shake my universe with a simple chat."

I want to tell him he is wrong; that you *can* shake someone's universe with a little chat because that is exactly what he did for me, but I don't.

"Look, you need help," he says. "Your dad—"

"Ex-dad."

"Right, ex-dad. If you need help in any way, or just wanna talk about it—"

The bell rings.

"So . . ." Gio says. He wants to know if I want to cut.

Since Gio isn't right about universe-altering chats, he can't be right about cutting, so I tell him, "No."

"Great," he says. "So you're gonna waste the whole day because of some insignificant bell that—"

This time I cut him off, because I want to be powerful and correct and win this argument, and even though I haven't thought it through by playing ping-pong in my head, I say it out loud: "What are you doing later?"

"No plans . . ."

"Come over for dinner, then. Phil will probably be there, so instead of telling you about Phil, I'll show him to you."

He smiles. "Mr. Head's golden rule."

"Exactly."

Since I am gaining trust in my ideas without playing ping-pong with them, I say, "Mr. Head rode into town on a big brown horse throwing gold nuggets of knowledge to hordes of screaming, happy children. I am the screaming, happy child in the back, gnawing on a turkey leg while stuffing gold in my brain."

"I don't get it," Gio says, "but I'll meet you here after school."

"After the *last* bell rings?" I ask, to make sure I understand.

"Ah, where would we be without bells?" he says, which is our inside joke.

"OKAY, CLASS, PUT YOUR READING JOURNALS IN THE BIN, so we can get started." Mr. Head's voice is clearer today. His eyes look clearer, too; they aren't foggy mirrors anymore. "Thank you for following directions. Today is a special day."

Yes, it is. Johnny Van Slyke isn't here. He has been suspended for one week for his "shenanigans," which is a funny word for "terrorizing me and Mr. Head."

However, Johnny's friend, Norman, the class Smartypants, isn't suspended. He sits in the back row with a maroon turtleneck, laughing his hyena laugh.

"Today is a very special day," Mr. Head says. "I am ready to start trusting you. I am ready for you to begin earning my trust. Yes, sir, I am ready."

Eight people roll their eyes, for a total of sixteen rolling eyeballs.

"Ready to start teaching you the mother of all classics, written by the father of drama, the God of wisdom, the blacksmith of iambic pentameter . . ."

Fourteen more eyeballs roll, two of which belong to

Norman, who says, "Okay, Head, I think we obviously get the point."

"That's *Mr.* Head," says Mr. Head.

"Okay, *Mr.* Head, I think we *obviously* get the point."

"If that's the case, then without further ado, I give you *Romeo and Juliet*."

Mr. Head turns on the television.

"But, Head, I mean, *Mr.* Head, *Romeo and Juliet* was *obviously* written as a play, not as a movie or a television show," Norman says, starting a wave of giggles. I, of course, don't giggle.

"Yes, Norman"—Mr. Head is using the tone of voice that my mom uses with me when she gets home from work—"*Romeo and Juliet* is indeed a play, but we must start somewhere. Since William Shakespeare's language is so antiquated, I'd like everyone to know the story line first. And I want everyone to see an example of dramatic irony, which is the literary device that we were studying when—"

Norman cackles. "When Johnny flipped on the strobe lights until Superman here flipped a desk."

"No, Norman," Mr. Head disagrees. "You mean when Johnny got himself suspended and Rene did what was difficult, did what was noble, did what was Shakespearean." He turns to me and nods his head in deep gratitude. "Although your cursing was unnecessary, I want to thank you, Rene, for your help." I feel like a superhero being honored at a city-wide parade. I try to act tough like a superhero, and not smile, but I can't, so guess I'm not a superhero.

Then I hear laughter from the back of the room, so loud and high-pitched that Norman the hyena falls off his chair, knees first, onto the dirty floor. "Maybe we all should leave you two alone," he chortles. "I'm sensing a Hallmark moment here."

"THAT WILL BE ALL, NORMAN," Mr. Head barks. "From you or from anyone else. My dignity and Rene's dignity are, and will *remain*, intact. Especially in this classroom. This will be a *safe* place . . . DO YOU UNDERSTAND?"

As Norman dusts himself off and returns to his chair, I hum "La Bamba" because Mr. Head is saving *me*—even aspiring superheroes need help *once* in a while—and because maybe Mr. Head no longer needs to be saved.

Norman looks down at his shoelaces. They are white with red stripes.

"What happened during last class is finished," Mr. Head continues. "The only carryover will be the point of that lesson, dramatic irony, which will be reinforced by the second half of the movie version of *Romeo and Juliet*. Is that clear, Norman?"

Norman's shoelaces are still white with red stripes.

"Good. I want everyone to pay attention to the use of dramatic irony. See if the audience knows something that the characters don't." Mr. Head pops in the DVD and skips to the second half of the film.

I don't know much about the God of wisdom, the blacksmith of iambic pentameter, or the father of drama, and I don't know why some movies deserve golden Oscars over others, but I do know that when Juliet wakes up from her nonpoisonous poison and sees Romeo dead and cold and alone, and then spots a knife, I want so badly for her to live that I stand up and shout, "No, Juliet, don't! You'll only make things worse!" which makes Norman laugh out loud which makes Mr. Head yell at him out loud which makes me proud to be Mr. Head's friend and in his room; and when Juliet kills herself and the two feuding families throw down their swords, I feel that moment of clarity and peace and understanding that only good movies like *Batman* and *Superman* and *Spider-Man* make you feel; so I clap, and since other students—even a few Bigbulletholes and Devilblackcoats—must feel that end-of-a-good-movie moment of clarity and peace and understanding, they clap, too.

"Hey, dunces," Norman snarls. "The actors *obviously* aren't here so they *obviously* can't hear you!"

"But, like, Norman," one Likegirl says, "it *was*, like, a great movie."

"Yeah, too bad it wasn't real . . . *of course*," he says.

I want to tell Norman that the movie *is* real because Ariel is my Juliet and I am her Romeo and one day we will run away together and I will need to escape poison in order to survive.

A knock on the door followed by a female voice. "Excuse me, Mr. Head, if I could pull Rene out for a few minutes, that would be great."

Yeah, great. It's Ms. Adelman, the school psychologist.

"Should he bring his stuff?" Mr. Head asks.

"Yes, that would be great."

Yeah, great. It's great when every student knows that I'm on my way to see the school shrink. It's great how thirty-two students stare at me as I pack up my pencils. It's great that it's so quiet that even Norman, who is squealing with delight under his rattlesnake breath, can hear me zip my backpack and swing it over my left shoulder.

It's great that the hallways are so quiet that I can hear my sneakers squeak and Ms. Adelman's heels clack with each step we take. Ms. Adelman is talking about small things, which is how she warms me up for bigger things when we reach her office.

"So, Rene, how was English today?"

"Fine."

"What were you learning?"

"Nothing."

"But I thought you liked Mr. Head."

Since she is no longer talking about small things, I put my finger over my lips, which is my secret code for "I don't want to talk when I'm not protected by security details like locks or walls or people I trust."

I see Gio peeking around the corner. This improves my security detail. "Rene, gotta run," he says, out of breath. "Not staying around till the bell, but I'm still in for tonight, if it's cool with you."

"Good afternoon, young man," Ms. Adelman says, which is, once again, just great. "I don't think we've met. I'm Ms. Adelman."

"Oh, hi there, Ms. Adelman. I'm Giovanni. Sorry to interrupt your, um, session, but I need to confirm plans with your client, Rene."

"That's excellent, Giovanni," she says, smiling like a bad actress in a bad movie.

"Right, uh, so anyway, when and where should I go, *Rene*?" he asks, emphasizing my name because I'm who he wants to talk to, which *is* great.

"134 Morningwell Avenue. 6:00 p.m. *sharp*."

"Anything else I should know?"

"Yeah, um, my dad—er, Phil—is a little, um . . ."

"Weird?"

"Uh, more like . . ."

"Corny?"

"Kind of but—"

"Embarrassing?"

"Yeah but—forget it. You'll see."

As Gio disappears down the hall, Ms. Adelman invites me into her office. I immediately start smelling my left hand and peeking at the clock to make sure we're not talking about anything important around the number thirteen. She settles into her chair and puts her feet up. The beige carpet still hasn't been cleaned.

"So, Rene, how are things going?"

"Fine."

"How are things with Mr. Head?"

"Fine."

"Not mad at him?"

"No."

"I heard you got pretty upset during class the other day."

"Did Mr. Head tell you that?"

"Yes. Does that upset you?"

"No."

"But you *were* upset during class . . ."

"You said it, not me."

"What made you so angry?"

"I wasn't angry."

"What's upsetting you?"

"Nothing."

"You look upset."

"You look like a forty-year-old lady with grandma glasses."

Ms. Adelman stares at me. I think she is angry at me for what I said about her glasses. I wait for her to speak. She doesn't. I count down from fifty, and she still hasn't said anything, which makes me nervous, even more nervous than usual, so I ask, "You want to look like a forty-year-old lady with grandma glasses?"

She smiles. "It's good that you're opening up."

"I'm not," I tell her so that she'll stop smiling.

"How's everything at home?"

"Fine."

"It must be strange having your father back."

"He's not my father," I object.

"What do you call him?"

"Phil."

"It must be strange having Phil in the house."

"Did Mr. Head tell you that?"

"Yes. Have you spoken to Phil?"

"Yes."

"And?"

"Gio will help me."

"Gio?"

"Giovanni. His friends call him Gio."

"Is Giovanni your friend?"

"Duh, that's why I call him Gio."

Ms. Adelman stares at me. I stare back. My mission is to not speak until she does. I don't have to wait long to end this mission because she asks, "What are you thinking about right now?"

"Eating dinner tonight with Gio and Phil."

"Well, that should be interesting."

"I guess."

"How does it make you feel?"

"It doesn't."

Ms. Adelman stares at me. I stare back. I begin another silent mission.

"What are you thinking right now?" she asks.

"That I want to leave."

"Your wish is granted."

"You should feel your abdominals tightening . . . Good . . . Breathe in through your nose and out through your mouth . . . Excellent."

I take the long way home so I don't have to be alone with Phil. When I finally get home, after fourteen laps around the neighborhood, Phil is still in his white underwear. The red hair on his chest and back and legs and feet hasn't disappeared.

He's wearing a white headband. It doesn't block any of the sweat dripping off him. On the television, a guy with curly hair and a big smile steps on and off a blue rectangle. "You should feel the burn in your quadriceps . . . Great job! Breathe in through your nose and out through your mouth . . . Excellent!"

Next to a half-empty bottle of water is an empty VHS case for *Buns of Steel.*

"Oh, hey, champ," Phil says, breathing hard.

Since I have no other choice, I say, "My friend is coming over." In other words, *this,* whatever *this* is, must become invisible within the hour or else I will run away, again, and wait on the corner for Ms. Donna and her yellow cheese bus to rescue me, again.

"Your mother . . . wants me to . . . relieve stress . . . and . . . get in shape," he says, between breaths.

And I want you to get a taxi and take it to China.

I don't say that. I never say stuff like that. You know, good comebacks, the ones that really bite. I'm terrible at them. I don't think of a good comeback until at least twelve seconds after I need it.

For instance, I didn't think of that taxi-to-China comeback until I was in my room, folding my clothes. I thought of storming into the living room and yelling back, "And I want you to get a taxi and take it to *China*!" but if I did, he'd have no idea what I was talking about. That's the thing about comebacks. They're now or never, like this dinner tonight.

It's now-or-never time for Phil. That's why I need Gio. I mean, I know what makes a good superhero—special powers, a burning desire to conquer evil, a name that ends in "man," a supermodel wife who loves the thrill of worrying about a superhero—but I don't know what makes a good dad. Or even a so-so dad. Or even a bad but acceptable dad, like the way microwavable meals make a bad but acceptable meal.

That's why I invited Gio. And that's why I need to convince my mom to let Gio come—not that it's going to be that hard. She'll probably want to buy me overinflated balloons and sparkly streamers and a chocolate ice cream cake with rainbow sprinkles when I tell her that I have a friend. Besides, my mom, as they say, is easy to push over.

As expected, when she walks in and I tell her that I invited a friend for dinner, she gives me one of those I'm-so-proud-of-you smiles like Ms. Adelman gives me when I tell her anything—like that I wish I could become invisible and run away.

My mom puts down her groceries and takes a deep breath. There are only a few small oranges and a head of lettuce in the bags so I know that she isn't breathing loudly because she is tired from carrying heavy groceries; she is breathing loudly because what she has to say is heavy.

I turn around and take two steps toward my room but she says, "We really need to talk, Rene. You, and me, and your father."

"You mean *Phil*," I correct her.

"No matter what he's done, he's still your father."

"His name is *Phil*."

She takes another deep breath. "There's a lot for us to discuss . . . together. You'll feel a lot better after we talk it over, I promise." She glances at her watch and sighs. "But I know your friend is coming over soon."

"Very soon. In less than an hour. My friend will be here at six o'clock sharp. Very sharp."

"Well, maybe after he leaves, we'll all clear the air."

"Maybe," I say, looking over at Phil.

Phil's buns don't look like steel, not that I looked—I mean, I did, but not like that. It was like driving past a car crash or walking through the *Ripley's Believe It or Not!* Museum: you know, shocking and sickening and therefore interesting. So, yeah, I watched as he turned off the tape, stretched while watching the movie *Dave,* then jogged to the bathroom.

Apparently, I'm more like Phil than I thought because songs get stuck in his head, too. All the way from my room, I can hear Phil singing in the shower: *Hail to the chief, he's the one we all say hail to, hail to the chief 'cause he keeps himself so clean . . . He's got the power, that's why he's in the shower.*

That's the thing about Phil: if you ignore everything else you see for fourteen years and simply focus on his shower songs, he seems like a swell guy.

I hope Gio brings his X-ray vision.

"Going for a walk, be back soon!" Phil yells.

"*Very* soon," my mom says. "Rene's friend will be here in about twenty minutes."

"Friend, huh? Well *that's* a first. I knew if I waited long enough—"

"Be nice! And be back soon!" she calls from her room.

"Okay, I'll see you soon, going for a quick walk." He shuts the door behind him.

"Instead of a quick walk, why don't you take a *hike*?" I mutter, twelve seconds too late.

THIS MOMENT, THIS MEETING OF FRIEND AND FOE, IS WHY my Batman cape was made. This is why the designer and the seamstress burned the midnight oil one cold night in China, weaving fabrics and colors together until finding the perfect blend of strength and beauty.

But my Batman cape is in the closet and that's where it will stay, at least until dinner is over. I can't wear it around strangers like Phil, who, unfortunately, should be home any second. I hope he gets lost on his walk, so lost that he accidentally ends up in China and marries the designer or the seamstress and lives in a small hut in a remote village without cell phones or pay phones or sailboats or cars or planes, so that he'll never be able to contact me again.

I don't realize I've been pacing my room, around and around and around like a caged orangutan, until I bump my right foot into the wall and stub my big toe. I rub the pain away with my right hand while checking the time. It's 5:56, which makes me nervous that Phil will be late, but optimistic that he'll run away. Again.

I walk over to the window. Still in the driveway is Phil's

red car, as bright and appalling as a fat pimple at the tip of my nose that must be popped: squeezed together, tugged apart, or both. Though it may bleed—and bleed it will, oozing down my cheek like melted strawberries and cream—it must be done; for he is my blemish, and he must go, leave, disappear into the night like Batman, lock himself in a Batcave and feed the key to a crazed colony of rabies-infested, squealing bats with vampire teeth and—

The front door creaks open. Phil's back. I look at my Batman watch: 5:59 and 58 seconds. "Honey, I'm home."

Honey? He better not be talking to me. Or my mom.

The doorbell rings at 6:00 and 11 seconds. I tear down the steps, but Phil is closest, so he answers the door.

Gio is wearing a navy blue sport jacket and dark blue jeans. His curly Afro is bent backward. It looks like a small bush after a storm.

Phil is dressed for the occasion in an orange tank top, the kind he used to wear to the beach. I, of course, am wearing a gray hooded sweatshirt in case the dinner gets ugly and I need to disappear.

Gio wipes his sneakers on the doormat and steps inside.

I wave at him. He waves back.

"Welcome," Phil says, shaking Gio's hand. "We've heard so much about you. It's so wonderful that I can finally put a face to a name."

This is a lie. Phil doesn't even know his name.

"Come on in, come on in," Phil says, patting Gio on the back and escorting him to the living room.

Gio nods politely. I wish Phil would take his hand off my best friend.

"Now if you'll excuse me for a second," Phil says. "Just need to fetch my—er, I'll be right back. Make yourself homely." He jogs into the kitchen.

Gio leans close to me and whispers, "He's not that bad."

I open my mouth to protest, but my mom's footsteps cut me off. Phil is a step behind her. My mom is out of breath, but her smile is as wide as I've ever seen. Specks of lipstick line her front teeth.

"You must be Gio," she says.

"That's me."

Phil chuckles. "*Gio* . . . such an interesting name. It sounds like Neo-Geo; you know, one of those fancy video game systems that Rene used to want."

How would you *know?* I say with my eyes.

"Anyway, thanks for coming over to our humble abode," Phil says. *Our* humble abode? This is *my* humble abode, not your humble abode. I want to shout this in Phil's face, but Gio looks so calm and I want him to feel comfortable in *my* humble abode.

"Doesn't look so humble to me, sir," Gio says, letting his eyes wander. "Nice house you have here."

I raise my eyebrows so Gio knows that Phil doesn't *have* a house here.

Gio adds, "And a very nice house you have here as well, Rene and Rene's mom."

"Ha! *Rene*'s *mom,*" Phil snickers.

My mom beams her Ms. Adelman's the-world-is-a-very-happy-place smile. "You are *so* polite, Gio," she says.

"Well, I was raised well. At an early age, my parents identified me as a child prodigy. They sent me to the finest schools, where they fed me only the finest meats and cheeses."

"Well, that explains it," Phil says, chuckling.

"Yes, that explains it," my mom echoes, smiling at Gio, then at Phil, then at me.

"Yes . . . that . . . does . . . explain . . . it," Gio repeats. "But in all seriousness, I taught myself to be polite."

My mom beams. "That's fantastic, Gio. How did you do it?"

"Practice. Lots of practice. I taught myself a lot of things. Had to learn to be independent. My mom . . . she worked, day and night. Still does, even in this new neighborhood of ours. I mean, of yours."

My dad smirks. "Well, it *is* a fine neighborhood we have here."

I shoot him a death stare, which unfortunately doesn't kill him.

"Yeah, I like it so far," Gio says. "Only been here a month and already I received a warm dinner invitation to eat with fine folks like yourselves. It's a pleasure to see such a close-knit family."

Everyone has white shoelaces, except for Phil, who isn't wearing shoes.

"Well, shall we?" my mom asks, pointing to the dinner table.

Gio and I sit on one side, Phil and my mom on the other.

"I'm famished," Phil says. "All that exercise really sparked my appetite."

And destroyed mine. I think of this comeback in perfect time, but I don't say it because we have company. I scribble a note in my mind to use it another time.

"You went for a run, sir?" Gio asks.

No, please no.

Phil grins. "Well, I actually worked up quite a sweat in this here living room."

"Oh, yeah? The old calisthenics routine of push-ups and sit-ups?"

I need to talk about small things so that the conversation doesn't lead to big things. "The weather is cold," I tell anyone who will listen.

Phil cracks his knuckles. "Just got back from a walk and didn't think it was too bad. But then again, I was still feeling the post-workout burn, which increases blood circulation and sweat volume."

I try again. "The food looks great."

"Corn on the cob and cold spaghetti," says Phil. "My, er, wife isn't such a great cook. Plus, can't pick more awkward foods to eat on a first date, huh, Gio? The corn sticks to your teeth—well, in your case, with your chipped tooth and all, it sticks to your *full* teeth, assuming you have at least *one* full tooth—and then the spaghetti never twirls the way you want, you know?"

I widen my eyelids so that Gio can see that I'm upset.

Phil looks at me and then back at Gio. "Where's your spaghetti shirt, Gio?"

I know what a spaghetti shirt is—so does my mom and obviously Phil does, too—but Gio doesn't know. Everyone knows but him. I think of Mr. Head, who would call this "dramatic irony." Phil laughs at Gio because he has no clue about spaghetti shirts.

If I were Gio, I would spend the rest of the night playing ping-pong with Phil's question: "Where's your spaghetti shirt?" . . . *What's wrong with me? Why don't I understand his question?* . . . "Where's your spaghetti shirt?" . . . *Where's* your *stupid spaghetti shirt?* . . . "Where's your spaghetti shirt?" . . . *I used it to clean the blood off your face after being a champ and knocking you out in the school parking lot.* Yeah, if I were Gio, that's what I'd say.

But I'm not Gio, who smiles politely and asks Phil to be more specific.

"Well, when we used to sit down and eat spaghetti, we made sure Rene wore red, so in case he slurped or spilled spaghetti sauce on himself—which, trust me, *always* used to happen and probably still *does* happen—the spaghetti sauce would blend in."

I grind my teeth. Forward and back, forward and back.

"A spaghetti shirt . . . I like that," Gio says.

"Me, too!" my mom shouts. "For years I've thought about marketing the idea. You know, sell a bunch of red T-shirts with 'Spaghetti Shirt,' written in different shades of red across the chest. I think thousands of parents would buy them, don't you?"

"Sure," Gio says. "You could sell it to old people, too. I know a couple of old fogies who *seriously* need spaghetti shirts." Gio winks at me because it's our inside joke.

"DON'T QUIT YOUR DAY JOBS!" Phil barks. "THE BOTH OF YOU!"

My mom tries to breathe but I don't think it's working.

"What do *you* do for a living, sir?" Gio asks, changing the subject. "Assuming you're not a fitness instructor."

"No, no," Phil says. "Not a fitness instructor—yet. No, I'm actually a writer."

"Oh, have you published anything?"

"Well, nothing yet, but the wheels of change are in motion."

"That's fantastic," Gio says. "What do you write?"

"Fiction, mostly, but I dabble in nonfiction every now and then."

"Anything in particular?"

My mom points at the dish in front of Phil and says, "Pass the corn, please."

Phil groans. I don't want them to argue so I pass her the corn. Phil turns to Gio. "Ever heard of the man, the myth, the legend—Mr. Bob Dylan?"

"You mean, Robert Zimmerman," I snigger.

"Zimmerman, Dylan, what difference does it make?" Phil fires back.

"He's right, Rene, look at our English teacher, *Richard* Head," Gio says.

Traitor. I should stab Gio in the back with a fork for siding with the enemy during mealtime.

Phil nods his head vigorously. "You know what, Rene, you'd be smart—for the first time in your life—to follow the advice of your wise friend," he says, looking at me with pity and at Gio with admiration (like everyone else does, including Richard Head). "You see," Phil continues, "this may sound corny and maybe a little too romantic for your young ears, but sometimes I stay up the whole night with headphones on, trying to come to terms with the fact that Bob Dylan is always right. Why is he always so *damn right* about everything? Life, love, friendship, justice, time . . . everything! He's always right!"

"Like you, sir," Gio says, smiling wide enough for me to see which other tooth I want to chip.

"Do you enjoy Bob Dylan's music, Gio?"

"You bet."

Phil smirks. "I *do* bet. A lot. Hard for me to stop."

"Oh."

"That's why I try to stay away from Atlantic City's casinos. Don't want to go down that road again. It's a dark road. With no headlights."

Gio looks over at me. I shrug.

Phil clears his throat. "Well, Gio, if you like Bob Dylan, you must be a writer."

"Of course."

"What a coincidence, two writers in the same room." Phil means that Gio and he are both writers. I am invisible, with or without my hood. "What genre do you prefer?"

"Poetry, mostly," Gio says.

"Poetry, eh? You know what they say about poets?"

That they're always on duty? That they feel crummy? That they have long faces?

"That they're geniuses?" Gio guesses, which sounds right because Gio said it.

"No, that they're psychos. Total psychotic psychos. I don't mean to burst your bubble or anything, but if you're interested in abnormal psychology, pick up a poetry anthology and read the biographies in the back. Suicide, despair, depression, divorce."

At the last word, my mom coughs into her palm and turns to me. "Want some more water, honey?"

She puts her hand on my knee, because she doesn't want me to get upset, raise my voice, make a scene—especially not a scary scene. I think of Ariel and breathe through my nose. It makes a whistling noise that sounds like "Twseeeet."

I unclench my teeth and tell my body not to do anything stupid. It doesn't listen. When I hold out my drinking glass for my mom to refill, I tell my fingers not to but they do it anyway: they relax, and let go.

The glass clanks on the table as water seeps into the white tablecloth.

"Way to go, champ." Phil laughs. "The food was too salty? That's why you diluted it?"

My mom presses her hand firmly on my knee.

I need to dilute you, I mutter to myself. Realizing my comeback makes no sense, I yell, *Way to go, dummy!* in my head, as I mop up the spill.

"Anyway, where were we?" Phil asks.

"Poets," says Gio.

"Right, psychos. Look, I don't mean to spoil your career or anything. You could turn out perfectly normal—then again, you *do* hang out with Rene here, who isn't exactly a model of mental hygiene."

I stop twirling my spaghetti. I tilt my fork until every noodle has slipped back onto my plate.

Phil says, "I mean, you gotta admit it, Gio. Rene ain't no social butterfly. I think you're the first friend he ever introduced me to"—My mom's fingernails dig deeper into my right knee—"Don't let me stop you, Gio. You wanna be a poet, be my guest. I'm sure you'll fit in just fine."

I try to stand up but my mom's fingernails are as sharp as knives.

"Who knows?" Phil shrugs. "You could fit in perfectly with other poets, Gio. You could be a psychotic, egomaniac, ultra-sensitive loony tune with a split personality. Hell, judging by the fact that you actually hang out with Rene, I'd bet the house that something is seriously wrong with you, champ."

"Gio isn't the psycho, you are."

Wait, did I just say that? What a comeback! But Phil heard it! Oh, God! No, wait, I'm glad he heard it!

"WHAT DID YOU *JUST SAY*?" Phil hollers. His eyes narrow.

I look at Gio. He nods.

"THAT'S IT!" I shout. "Gio's not a psycho; I'm not a psycho either. There's nothing wrong with me. Well, maybe some things, but at least I don't treat people like, like dirt. YOU'RE THE PSYCHO!"

My hands are shaking.

"Mom," I say. "Phil needs help."

Phil looks like an angry bull. Invisible smoke flows from his nose.

I stand up, point a finger at Phil, and yell, "GET OFF MY BISCUIT!" Then, leaving no trace as to where I'm going or how long I'll be gone, I kick open the front door.

Gio follows.

It's 8:09 on a breezy Wednesday night. A school night. My block is deserted. So is the one after that and the one after that. A soccer ball rests against the curb, but nobody chases after it. Fireflies blink through the night, but nobody captures them. The grass smells like a #2. A television flickers in someone's house.

My hands are shaking like an old man's hands. I bury them in my pockets. I can still feel them quivering against my thighs. I should be home now. I should be in my room, thinking of cereal and Ariel and rescuing Mr. Head (again), but if I go home now, there's no way I could go to my room because my mom and Phil won't want to talk about small things.

There'd be a long conversation with Phil about why he's here and how I feel about that, and then, of course, the next conversation will be about Gio and how his bad influence has caused me to disrespect Phil, who, as my mom will say, is *still* my father; and then at the end of the whole talk, when the clock has already struck midnight, Phil will say, "You told me to get off your biscuit, and since I like to be in touch with today's lingo because of my writing career, what exactly is a 'biscuit'?" which will be hard for me to answer because I don't really know, so then Phil, like Norman and the rest of the Smartypants kids at school, will say, "You called me that and you don't even know what it means? You *really* don't know what it means? Hah, you *really* don't know!"

I assume that "biscuit" means something sexual, because most words that I don't understand have something to do with sex. For instance, in the fifth grade, Johnny Van Slyke's friend Norman went around calling everyone a scrotum. Because it was a word that made everyone laugh, I knew it had to be something sexual.

But it's not *always* like that. Later that year, he was the one who went around telling everyone their epidermis was showing. So, of course, I checked my zipper. That's when he pointed his finger at me and said, "You *really* don't know what that means?"

The more I think about sexual stuff and Smartypants kids and everything I don't know, the harder it is for me to go home tonight. Besides, I want Phil to worry so that his head and neck and shoulders will be heavy from stress like mine have been for the past six years—and I want my mom to worry so she'll think twice about having Phil at home. That's why I'm glad I didn't bring my cell phone. Let them worry. Let them reconsider what they've done and what they've said. Let them sweat it out, and when they're on the verge of dying of dehydration from sweating so much, *I'll* call *them*.

I can make it on my own. I mean, it's not like my mom tucks me in my own bed *every* night. I've already spent a night away from my bed—even if it was by accident.

Gio punches me in the arm. "So what's the plan, Stan? Forget it. What's the plan, *Rene*?"

I tell him all the reasons I can't go home.

"I don't blame you, brother man. That Phil, what a character! Jesus H. Christ!"

"Jesus *Harry* Christ."

"Right. You know how they say that a person can be like an onion, and that you gotta peel away the layers to get to know who they really are?"

I nod.

"Well, that Phil ain't no layered onion. I know I just met the dude, but you know what he's like?"

I shake my head because I want Gio to tell me what Phil is really like so that I can tell my mom when I eventually go home to rescue her.

"Phil is like a hard-boiled egg that won't peel," Gio explains. "You know, you smash it on the table so that the shell shatters into tiny pieces that are still connected like a spiderweb. But then, when you try to peel the pieces away, you realize that they're stuck and that you can't peel anything. That's what Phil is: a hard-boiled egg that doesn't peel."

"Phil *is* a hard-boiled egg."

"So what are you gonna do about your hard-boiled egg? Smash it, scrap it, or eat pancakes?"

"Anything but pancakes," I say, picturing Phil's chest hairs sizzling on the skillet.

"Seriously, what are you gonna do?"

I shrug my shoulders.

Headlights glare in the distance, as a car accelerates down a hill and swerves to the left. "Hide!" I yell, and run behind a tree, in case it's Phil or my mom looking for Gio and me.

As the car approaches, two Cutters from school stick their heads out the window and yell "Whooooo! Yeahhhhh!" The car swerves to the right and then speeds away.

My heart is racing as fast as that car, but at least it wasn't Phil behind the wheel. When I catch my breath, I tell Gio that I have no idea what to do next.

Gio puts a hand on my shoulder. "Look, it's complicated, brother man. I feel that. Stress can be a debilitating little bugger, but you know what they say about stress, right?"

"That it comes from end-of-shower bad-luck water?"

He frowns. "No, that it's fight or flight."

"I want to fly but I left my Batman cape in my closet at home."

"Look, brother man, let's be serious here for a minute, huh?"

Gio's right. No Batman cape. It'd be impossible to run into the house and grab it without having that conversation about big things with Phil and my mom.

"Why don't you sleep over at my house?" he says. "It's right down the street."

REMEMBER HOW I SAID THAT GIO'S HOUSE LOOKS LIKE NAture? That was in the daylight, when its green and brown shutters made it look like a semi-healthy tree. In the dark, it's a swamp. Hornets buzz around a rotten apple, maggots gnaw on what's left of a dead squirrel. And although I can't see them, there are probably lice out there, too, those invisible bugs the school nurse removed from my hair with chopsticks back in kindergarten.

I throw my hood on to block the lice. By the time we reach the front steps, I'm convinced that I already *have* lice, which is doomsday because by the looks of Gio's house, he probably doesn't have any chopsticks lying around.

I reach inside my hood and scratch at my scalp until I feel blood on my nails, which means that I either decapitated the lice or sliced my head open. My head is throbbing. Calling a doctor isn't an option, because he'd call my parents, so I press as hard as I can on my scalp to stop the bleeding but I don't think it's working. I press harder and harder and my head hurts more and more which means that—

"You okay?" Gio asks.

"When we get inside, I need to go to the bathroom."

Gio turns the key and the front door creaks open like a scary scene in a scary movie that I am in and therefore can't press Pause.

"Make yourself at home," he says. "My mom's not here, for a change. Always working, never calling. I don't even *know* where my sister is. If you're still hungry I could—"

"Bathroom. Please." My scalp is on fire.

"The bathroom is the second door on the right. Make sure not to step on Rufus."

"Rufus?"

"Yeah, my dog."

"Dog!" I shout in my head but whisper to Gio. *My allergies, my asthma!*

"Yeah, Rufus sleeps on the floor downstairs out here, so that he doesn't bother the cats I keep in my room."

"Cats!" I gasp.

"Yeah, we have four of them."

"Four cats!"

"Yeah, they sleep in my room so they don't torment the guinea pig in my sister's room."

"Guinea pig!"

"Yeah, I know, I keep telling her that guinea pigs are gross, but she begged my mom for years until she finally gave in. What a weasel."

"Weasel!"

He chuckles. "Yeah, sneaky as hell. Hey, you sure you're okay?"

"Where's the bathroom again?"

"Second door on your right, but watch out for Rufus."

I run to the bathroom and leap over Rufus and his deadly hair and saliva, and then lock the door to the bathroom and crumple into a ball.

I take three deep breaths—which don't come easily because my windpipe feels like it's closing—and *then* think. I think I can't breathe *(sniffle)*. I think I can't stay *(sneeze)*. I think my eyes are burning *(sneeze)*. I think I'm wheezing *(croak)*. I think I'm going to suffocate *(croak)*. I think I'm already suffocating *(croak)*.

I stand up without touching anything with my hands and look in the mirror. I look fuzzy, not because there's fog in the mirror but because there's fog in my eyes. Red streaks and red clouds fill the whites of my eyes; it looks like the devil crawled inside them and stuck them with his pitchfork. Through the clouds, I can see that my scalp is bleeding, not a whole lot but there's blood in my hair and blood on my fingers and blood under my nails. I wipe it on my hands and try to—

Breathe! I think I can't stay *(sniffle)*. I think I sound like Mr. Chalmers *(sniffle)*. I think I have nowhere else to go *(sneeze)*. I think I'm stuck *(sniffle)*. I think I'm trapped *(sneeze)*. I think this is doomsday.

Someone's tapping on the door.

I close my eyes. There are thousands of ping-pong balls in my head and I only have one racket. The local police chief just got word of my escape. He is mobilizing a search party and preparing to release the hounds.

"Rene, did you fall down the toilet, brother man?"

I am homeless. I should break into school and sleep on Mr. Head's desk again if Mr. Head isn't sleeping there already. I need to go #1/pee/piss/urinate/drain the monkey/empty my bladder/drizzle. I have only nine lives and I'm wasting one of them tonight.

"You all right, Rene?"

If I keep smelling my left hand, my nose will run out of air and I will die of asphyxiation and Rufus will be charged with murder but it will be difficult to handcuff him and bring him to trial so Gio will be charged with murder and grilled by the Feds who will blow cigarette smoke in his face before they throw him in jail.

"Yo, Rene, seriously, you all right in there?"

How will anyone identify me if nobody knows me? Gio said that people know me but he was lying. I should have made more friends.

"Rene, yo, Rene!"

This is not a noble way to die. Noble deaths are stupid anyway because every dead man has the same thing in common. My armpits smell like raw onions and rotten fish. I didn't bring deodorant and can't buy any now because I am broke and homeless and will soon be dead. Having Gio over for dinner was a terrible idea.

"Rene, if you don't open this door, I'm gonna break it down!"

I wish I were Mr. Head; I wish I were Mr. Chalmers; I wish I were anyone but me—anywhere but here.

"Rene, I'm counting down. Here I go: 5 . . . 4 . . ."

That countdown is the death knell which is the intro music for a wrestler named The Undertaker.

"3 . . ."

I locked the door, thank God I locked it. I'm sorry for believing in God only during difficult times; I know it's petty and phony but it's human nature to be a Smartypants.

"2 . . ."

I open the door.

Gio takes one look at me and pulls me out of the bathroom, then shoves me out the front door. Lice and maggots and hornets scratch and bite into me, but I fight through like a young warrior with an iron heart and a mighty sword. I swat at my enemies and make it through the battlefield.

"You should have told me you're allergic!" Gio yells, pulling me onto his lawn.

"I don't have anywhere else to go," I explain.

"You don't know *anyone else* without a dog?"

"No."

"No relatives?"

"Just mom."

"Grandparents? Uncles? Aunts? Godparents?"

"None, but . . . what about Edith and Milton? Maybe we can stay with them."

"Yeah, right. You know how much money it costs to stay there?"

"No."

"More than a hotel."

"Oh, well we—we could sleep on their floor."

Gio holds his breath. I am convinced that we'll be sleeping on the floor as Milton and Edith snore and drool and fart next to us—until Gio says, "Brother man, that place has more cameras than a convenience store."

Because I have no more ideas, I say, "I have no more ideas."

"Me neither," he says. "Looks like you got yourself caught in a pickle jam."

"Do you know how to get out of a pickle jam?"

"Not *this* pickle jam," Gio says, "unless—"

"Unless what?"

He puts a hand on my shoulder. "Unless we run away."

I don't cut class. I don't pull fire alarms. I don't like to curse. I don't run away.

"You want to go back to Phil's house?" Gio suggests.

"It's *my* house," I snap, tossing Gio's hand off me. "It's my humble abode."

"Well, it seems like it's *his* house now."

"IT IS NOT!!!" I say this so loud that my eyes water. I cover my face with my bloody fingers and bloody nails.

"I'm sorry, Rene. I didn't mean to . . ."

Back at my house, Phil is laughing at my bloody fingers and bloody nails as he twirls his spaghetti. He is making fun of the fact that I used to wear spaghetti shirts. He is telling my mom that I still need a spaghetti shirt because my fingers and nails are covered in red.

"I really am sorry, Rene."

I put my hands inside my pockets.

"Look, today is Wednesday," Gio says. "Well, tomorrow is Thursday and then we have Friday off. It would only be for a few days."

"Where would we go?"

"Anywhere, brother man. Anywhere but here. Sound good to you?"

"Yeah, but—"

"But what?" Gio asks.

"But school."

"We only have one more day this week. This Friday is a teacher in-service, a day for teachers to sit around and talk smack about kids, and then it's the weekend. We'd only miss one day."

"Yeah, but—"

"But what?"

"But my mom and her search party: dogs with vampire teeth and a superhuman sense of smell, flashlights burning through the night until they find me; and when they find me they will—"

"Yo, you're talking about the same mom who disappeared this past week."

"That's true."

"We could take a bus to a city," he says.

"New York City?"

"Any city. As long as it has three things."

"Right: fireflies, privacy, and superheroes," I say.

"I was thinking more like girls, diversity, and street vendors."

"Those, too."

"So . . . ?" Gio says, which means that he wants an answer.

Since I'm not highly skilled at making decisions, I sit on Gio's stoop for six hours, picking at lice and dozing off and playing ping-pong with the idea of running away.

And then I stand up.

THE STREETS ARE DARK AND NAKED. I COULD DISAPPEAR now and nobody except Gio would even notice.

It would be hard to disappear, though, because two black T-shirts, two pairs of socks, a toothbrush, and a notebook are hanging from my back, stuffed into Gio's spare green backpack. I know that it's Gio's backpack and not his sister's because "Giovanni" is written underneath the label for L.L.Bean. Gio's eyes are focused straight ahead. He is my fearless leader. I think about asking him if his bold, adventurous spirit was passed down from generation to generation in his family like awkwardness and ugliness and compulsiveness were passed down in mine, but I don't want to ask him anything right now because I may not like the answer.

(For the same reason, I don't want to ask him where he got the $200 that he stuffed in his pocket as we left his house; where we'll sleep; whether he knows where we're going; and I definitely don't want to ask him "Are we there yet?" because every time I asked Phil that question on our way to Monticello—Jefferson's old, white house—he would pull over and punch the steering wheel for ten minutes before restarting his car.)

Besides, the silence feels good. The ping-pong balls have stopped bouncing off one another. It's 5:30 a.m., and the streets, as I said, are dark and naked, and the houses pretty much look the same. Same shape, same shutters. I wish school were like this so that I wouldn't have to throw a hood over my head to make myself invisible. Maybe someday, if I make it to college, all of the classes will be held at night with the lights turned off so that nobody can see the difference between me and the guy next to me.

Maybe Mr. Head will teach one of my classes. He'll know that I don't like to be called on so he won't call on me. Then again, the classes will be in the dark, so maybe I'll actually *want* to be called on. Maybe I'll even come to the front of the room and give oral presentations and take questions from the class. Everyone will be so impressed that they'll ask to be my study partner. Maybe some people will even ask for my autograph or my business card or my secret identity.

Until then, I need to keep walking—and show Gio that I'm not scared. A few fireflies wink at me, which makes me feel better, but I can already hear the police chief convincing my mom that it's okay for his search party to "sic the dogs" on me . . . I can see Mr. Head taking attendance in the morning with puddles of sweat on the back of his shirt because he doubts I'm still alive . . . I can feel Phil's anger breaking glass . . . and I can smell rotting banana peels and stale pizza because there are Dumpsters next to the Greyhound bus station, which is lit up like fireworks on a summer night, with independence and freedom and fear at my fingertips.

There's no fear on Gio's fingertips. Leaving town is his destiny. His mission. I play ping-pong with the thought that this trip is *his* mission, not mine. This makes me feel worse.

My eyes are burning as we approach the station. Two snack machines and one soda machine are almost but not completely naked: a red "Sorry, but I'm broken" sign is taped on the front of each one.

The bus terminal, however, isn't naked. There are fifty-eight people waiting inside, twenty-five of whom are sitting in blue seats that look about as comfortable as sitting Indian style on a pile of glass.

"So, where to, Rene?" Gio asks, which is the first thing he has said in forty-two minutes and fourteen seconds.

"I don't want to sit on those blue seats," I tell him.

"No, I mean, where to? You know, which city?"

I don't want to be the one who decides because that's the person who takes all the blame if everything falls apart. "You decide," I say. "Which city has the most, er, girls, diversity, and street vendors?"

"It's a no-brainer," he says. "If you're leaving it up to me, New York City it is."

"Okay, let's go there."

Gio buys the tickets as I wait in line for the New York City bus. There are thirty-six other people in line, thirty-three with faces so tired they look like survivors of a scary scene in a scary movie, and three girls, two with tall yellow backpacks, who won't stop talking. They each have long hair, but all different colors: brown, blond, and red. Even though I can't see their faces because they're at the very front of the line and I'm at the very back, I can hear every word they say:

Brown hair: "New York *is* a melting pot, but I don't like what it all melts into."

Blond hair: "I know what you mean. It's like the snow. It looks all nice and pretty until it becomes a pile of salt and sand."

Red hair: "Be grateful! We're going to *New York City.* Get excited!"

Brown hair: "Oh, come on. You sound like a groupie. Promise me you'll never become one of those people who moves to a city and falls in love and never leaves."

Red hair: "It's not *a* city. It's *the* city."

Brown hair: "You don't actually *believe* that . . ."

Blond hair: "What do you expect? She hasn't traveled nearly as much as we have. She hasn't even left the country, for crying out loud. I mean, she hasn't even been to a spiritual place like Machu Picchu. I bet she doesn't even know what country Machu Picchu is in."

Red hair: "I *do, too.* It's in Peru."

Brown hair: "Hah! She said, 'Per-oo!' Typical American pronunciation."

Blond hair: "She doesn't even roll her 'R's!'"

[Blond hair and Brown hair laugh at, not with, Red hair.]

I want to think of a comeback for Red hair to say but I

don't use comebacks on strangers because you never know how psycho people can be. Phil taught me that.

Gio comes back with the tickets. "We don't save any money buying round-trip, so I figured we'd get two one-way tickets, just in case we're able to hitch a ride home with somebody; and if our journey takes us to another city, we don't want to have to backtrack. Besides, a one-way ticket gives you the illusion you're leaving for good. Wouldn't you agree?"

"Sounds fine." I wipe my burning eyes with the backs of both hands.

"I think we've found somewhere for you to sleep," Gio says. "The bus leaves at 6:00 and doesn't get into New York City until 8:15, so unless there are a bunch of big mouths, you should sleep like a baby."

I gesture over my shoulder toward Brown hair and Blond hair, so that Gio knows that sleep won't come easy.

"Next stop, New York City. Have all tickets out please," the bus driver announces. He's wearing a name tag that says, "Hello, my name is Ron."

Ron the bus driver starts ripping people's tickets, and as each person files onto the bus, I am convinced that there won't be any seats left, which means that I'll have to sleep on the blue concrete seats and wait for the next bus—assuming I still want to go by then, but I don't think I will because the sun will be out and everybody knows that in the light of day nobody does anything reckless and stupid and spontaneous like run away to New York City, which means I'll have to go back and talk to Phil and grab my stuff and wait for Ms. Donna to pull up in her cheese bus and—

"Yo, brother man, it's your turn," Gio says. I realize that although the line has moved, I haven't.

"Any day now, son," Ron grumbles.

"My bad," Gio says. "Sorry about that, sir."

Ron rips our tickets. "Look to the back of the bus for seats."

Ron is right. There are only four empty seats, in the back.

As I walk past each stranger, I write their stories in my head: the bald guy in the front row recently got fired, his marriage is failing; the elderly lady in the second row is visiting her grandkids in New York City; the guy in the blue suit is on his way to a job he can't stand; the middle-aged man with an unkempt beard had a ham and cheese sandwich for breakfast, now his stomach hurts; Blond hair is deathly allergic to peanuts; Brown hair is on her fourth trip to New York City this month; and Red hair . . . she's . . . Red hair is . . . my . . . she's . . . I force myself to breathe in deeply so the scent of red roses stays with me the entire bus ride as I dream of an Angel, my Angel, my Ariel.

22

"YOU WANT THE AISLE OR THE WINDOW?" GIO ASKS.

Ariel is here. On this bus. With me. She's running away. Like me. Like Romeo. Like Juliet. Gio will be our friar. He will marry us on top of a mountain. The wedding will be a secret. The only people there will be me, Ariel, Gio, and Mr. Head. As a respectable elder and public authority figure, Mr. Head will certify the wedding. But nobody else. Ariel and I both want it that way. She'll need to escape Brown hair and Blond hair and their yellow backpacks and all the jealous Angels back at Radcliffe High School.

From the front of the bus, heavy breathing into a microphone: "Good evening, or should I say, 'Good morning'? My name is Ron and I'll be your driver this evening, er morning. There's no smoking in the coach and no . . ."

"Yo, Rene, you want the aisle or the window?" Gio asks again.

How will I propose to her? Should I do it at the beach or at a classy restaurant like Wendy's? Not at McDonald's, of course. She deserves the best. And everyone knows that a Wendy's chocolate Frosty puts you in the mood for love, as long as you don't eat/drink the whole thing. I'll go down on one knee when she's halfway through the Frosty—on the beach, that's where I'll do it. It'll work. It has to work. I'll freeze the Frosty and take it with us to the beach at night, and when she's halfway done with her Frosty and her heart is warm and her brain is cold, I'll put one knee in the wet sand and say, "Ariel, will you marry me?"

Gio taps me on the right shoulder. "Yo, brother man, are you gonna stare at the seat or sit in it?"

"Oh, sorry."

"Aisle or window?"

"Aisle." Obviously I get a better view from the aisle.

"Fine with me," he says. "The window's better for sleeping and writing."

Ariel's red hair hangs to the right of her aisle seat six rows ahead of us. I have two hours and fifteen minutes to stroll up the aisle and convince her to come with us.

It'll be easy. I'll stand up, stroll sixteen paces and wave. She'll wave back. I'll ask, "Do you want to come with us?" She'll say, "Yes, thank you for saving me from my Smartypants friends; I would love to come with you and Gio." Then I'll ask, "How did you know I was with Gio?" and she'll say, "I saw you both come on the bus, but I was too shy to look at you." I'll say, "Ariel, you're an Angel," and she'll start crying and I'll get scared, so she'll comfort me by saying, "Don't be frightened, Rene. I'm crying out of happiness." Since I'll feel happiness, too, I'll cry, too. She'll shove her Smartypants friends out the window so we can sit and cry together. We won't have any tissues to wipe our tears or blow our noses on, so we'll rub our boogies on each other, or on each other's sleeves, which won't bother Ariel because she's an Angel.

I crane my neck so that I can see as much of her hair as possible. *I can do this. I can do this. Once the bus starts moving, I'll do it.* The bus starts moving. *Once the bus reaches that traffic light, I'll do it.* The bus reaches that traffic light. *Once the traffic light turns green, I'll do it. It'll be like giving our relationship a green light.* The traffic light turns green. *Okay, this is it. Once we cross the bridge, I'll do it. It'll be a magic bridge between childhood and adulthood, single life and marriage, misery and ecstasy.* We cross the bridge. I am still single and miserable and a child.

I slump back in my seat. Gio doesn't seem to notice; he's writing in a notebook. I don't want to talk about big things like marrying Ariel, so I ask him what he's writing.

"Poetry," he says.

Remembering our dinner conversation, I tell him, "I don't think poets are psychos."

"Thanks."

"What do you write about?" I ask.

"I'd rather show you instead of tell you."

"Right. Mr. Head's golden rule."

He smiles. "Exactly."

"So show me."

"I want to," Gio says. "But I've never really shown my writing to anyone before. It makes me feel kind of—"

"Naked?"

"Well, yeah," he says.

"I promise I won't laugh at you."

"I know you won't. In fact, here." He hands me his notebook. "Read the first one."

The sun is just starting to rise, but it's still dark inside the bus, so I turn on the overhead light, get comfortable in my seat, and focus my eyes . . .

Gray Suburbia
by Gio Caperna

I can't describe any snow-capped mountains
Or ripe mangoes hanging over white sand
I can tell you what a tear tastes like but I can't
Describe early morning narcolepsy stalking
My eyelids after working three jobs through the night
Alone shivering at a cash register I can't
Tell you about riding the subway sweating
Out of cash gripping the railing afraid I'll miss
My stop my girlfriend sleeping on my thigh but I can
Tell you what rain smells like in summer and
I can explain Newton's gravitational laws
But I can't describe stars on a clear night or
Crickets jazzing away at dusk or even a
Sunset leaning on a skyscraper I never
Turned to the ocean as a companion but I do
Know what minimum wage means and I understand

That everyone needs to go to college and I can
Describe inspiration running faster than it came but
I don't know the difference between Monday and Thursday and
I've never followed a charismatic leader because
I only see them on the history channel and hear about them
From my mother who makes dinner cleans up does laundry
She asks me how school was I say fine but it's not because
I can't describe the clubs in Manhattan red white and
Blue lights shining over a man with wide shoulders
Ignoring my fake ID and wide eyes I can't
Tell you if Kentucky bluegrass is really blue
Or if it changes color through the seasons I can
Tell you about science fairs and spelling bees
And British poets and Christopher Columbus
And friendships forever buried under the current
Of girls with dimples and brown hair and
I can tell you about proms and social politics and
All the movies coming out this winter
But I can't claim any responsibility for my being here
In gray suburbia writing about what never
Happened and what did

"Whoa, how long did that take you?" I ask.

"Brother man, don't ask me that."

"Why not?"

"Because writing isn't measured in time. Sometimes your brain is jammed up like a new ketchup bottle and you can't get *anything* out, not one single sentence, no matter how hard you bang on it; other times the words flow smoothly and effortlessly and deliciously like Mountain Dew from an ice-cold fountain."

"That's how I feel!"

"Seriously?"

"Yeah, except the last part," I tell him. "Words don't flow like Mountain Dew for me. Ever."

"It takes practice. The more you write, the better you get."

"I didn't know you're a poet, Gio."

He frowns. "I'm *not* a poet. Writing poetry doesn't make me a poet."

"Why not?"

"Because poets get published. And have names."

"I don't understand."

"You know, famous names."

"Like Bob Dylan?" I ask.

"Kind of. But even though they're famous, they only eat rice."

"Why rice?"

"Because they're poor," he says.

"Like you?"

"Yes, like me."

"But not like Bob Dylan."

"No, not like Bob Dylan. Real poets sleep in gutters."

"Because they're poor?" I ask.

"No, because sleeping in gutters makes you want to write."

"I don't get it."

"Sleeping in gutters gives you something to write about," Gio explains.

"You mean like us sleeping on a bus at six o'clock in the morning?"

"Kind of."

"You mean like us running away and using fake ID's to get into nightclubs?"

"Kind of."

"I don't get it."

"Do you write, brother man?"

"I do my reading journals for Mr. Head's class."

"No, I mean *write,* like *really* write."

"Are you asking me if I'm a writer?"

"I'm asking if you write because you want to . . . because you have to . . . because if you don't, your brain will explode into a million bloody pieces," Gio says.

I squirm in my seat. My butt is sore from sitting for so long. "I actually want to be a writer," I tell him. "Phil is a writer."

"That's why you want to be a writer?"

"No."

"Well then, why?"

"Because there are always things that I think of and want to write down on little scraps of paper or Post-its or receipts."

"Right! Exactly. That happens to me, too. If I don't write it down, I'll forget. It's like, I'll have a thought—a crashing wave into a pit of sand—but it disappears before I even see it fill."

"That's deep," I say. Gio sounds like a wise man sitting Indian style on top of a frosty mountain.

"I have to write stuff down on something—anything!—so that my thoughts don't disappear."

"That's what Phil does and he's a writer."

"You're killing me, brother man."

"I don't want to kill you—yet," I say, which makes Gio laugh.

"I don't mean to pry," he says, "but it sounds like you want to be a writer because of Phil."

"I don't. I mean—"

"Say no more, brother man." Gio sighs. "I get it. I really do."

"Get what?"

"I get it. We all go through it, brother man. We don't like our fathers, sometimes we don't even *respect* them, but we still want to please them. We want their approval. We want desperately for them—who we aren't proud of and don't even respect—to be proud of and respect us. Brother man, I'd wrestle an alligator—I'd fight a bear, a grizzly bear with sharp claws and an insatiable hunger—for my father to say, just once, 'Son, I'm proud of you,' even though he was a drunk who walked out on my mom before I was born."

"Why do you care about him so much?"

"Same reason you do. Same reason you want to be a writer—though I think you'd be damn good at it either way."

"You really think so?"

"I do. You know what else I think?"

"That I'm smarter than Phil?"

"I already thought that."

"Then what were you thinking?"

"That you've got your eye on someone on this bus."

Ron the bus driver honks at a car in front of him.

"Does she have blond, brown, or red hair?" Gio asks me.

"I don't—"

"Save it, brother man. You were almost fallin' out of your seat before."

"I-do-not-love-anyone," I say, sounding like a robot.

"But you were nervous earlier."

I nod.

"Were you nervous about something?"

I shake my head.

"Someone?"

The last time I looked in Gio's eyes to see if Ariel was swimming in them, I was sitting next to Milton. I didn't see her then and I don't think I see her now, but if Ariel really *is* swimming in Gio's eyes, I don't want Gio to know that I am in love with her. Besides, telling Gio about Ariel means I'll actually have to talk to her, which means I'll have to look at her when she's talking to me, and look at her when I'm talking to her, and she's going to look at me and stare at me while talking to me and waiting, in vain, for me to respond.

"So," he says, "which one is it?"

"The red-haired one. The Angel."

"*Angel,* eh? That's quite a compliment."

"It's an understatement."

"So what's the holdup? Why won't you talk to her?"

"I . . . Because . . . She's . . . I'm . . ."

"Come on, brother man. Talking to strangers is easy. You got nothing to lose."

"She's not a stranger!" I hiss, then regret it. I suck in air to take back my words.

"Damn, brother man. You're in deep already."

The guy in front of me tilts his chair so far back that it's almost in my lap. "You all right, brother man? You want me to tell this guy to—"

"No, I'm fine."

"Let me know if you get uncomfortable. Now back to the girl. How do you know her?"

"From school."

"Our school?"

I nod. "Our school . . . our year."

"What's she doing here?"

"What are *we* doing here?" I ask, which makes Gio laugh.

"Maybe she's running away, too," he suggests.

"Or maybe she knew we would be here."

"You think she's a spy or something, brother man?"

"No, I mean maybe it's meant to be. Like in the movies."

"'Rene the romantic.' I think I'll call you that from now on, if you don't mind."

"I'm not a romantic. I've never *been* a romantic. The last time I had a girlfriend was in the third grade."

"How'd you meet her?"

"In gym class. She was chasing me."

Gio laughs. "Chasing you with what?"

"A monkey's head."

Gio laughs even louder. "Why was she chasing you?"

"Maybe she just enjoyed a good chase."

"*Enjoyed a good chase?* That's it?"

"Yup."

"I don't buy it. There's got to be more to it."

"All right, I ripped the head off her stuffed animal, so she chased me with it."

"And?"

"And since then, no girlfriends. I just freeze up, because I—I get . . ."

"You get scared."

I nod.

"Girls aren't as scary as they look," he says. "They're like us, except they smell better."

"And look better and talk better and smile better and walk better."

"And, they're sweeter," he says.

"And nicer," I add.

"Most of the time," Gio says. "See, I'm sure this red-haired chick—"

"She's not a chick!" I yell, which makes the guy in front of us say, "Shushhhh."

"Chill out, loser," Gio tells him. The guy makes this sound: "Hrrrrumph."

"She's not a chick," I whisper. "Her name's Ariel Merriweather."

"Okay, you know her name, that's a start. Does she know yours?"

"You said everybody at school knows me."

Gio takes a deep breath through his mouth. "Well, they do. I'm sure she knows you. You'll be fine. Just do your thing."

"What's my thing?"

"You know, be yourself."

"I don't think that's a good idea."

"Maybe not," he says. "But it's who you are."

My shoelaces are gray. And dirty. I should wash my hands *at least* four times but the bathroom on the bus is probably dirtier than my hands, so maybe I should—

"Go!" he says, nudging me.

My left hand smells like cat fur.

I have one last question, and since my mom taught me to ask questions whenever I am unsure, I turn to Gio and whisper, "If Ariel and I want to get married in a few days, will you be our friar?"

I AM STANDING IN THE MIDDLE OF THE AISLE. ANY SECOND now, Ron the bus driver will order me to sit down. I will tell him, "No."

The sky is navy blue with purple streaks. It is beautiful, but not as beautiful as Ariel. The sun is rising fast. I need to do this, and I need to do it now.

Sixteen paces in front of me, Ariel twirls her hair with her left index finger. She is waiting for me, ready to take my hand and whisper her vows in my ear.

My left hand smells of corn on the cob and spaghetti. It smells of Phil. It smells of dog saliva. It smells of Gio's clothes.

I try to move forward, but I am standing in quicksand. My feet and ankles and legs are shrinking faster than Milton and Edith.

My left hand smells like last summer. It smells of lost caterpillars and dead fireflies. It smells of being alone.

The bus breaks sharply and veers to the right. Everyone, except for me, shifts in their seats. I am still standing, but sinking fast.

"Hickory, dickory, dock, the mouse ran up the clock. The

clock struck one . . . Lunch!" *Tell her that, even though it's not lunchtime.*

My left hand is quivering.

"Can I sit with you? Can we grow old together?" *Say that!*

"Hi, Ariel Merriweather, you look good in any type of weather." *Tell her that!*

A microphone crackles. "In the back, sit down please."

I jump back into my seat before Ariel can see me. Or *did* she see me? Did she recognize me? Does she even know I exist?

I close my eyes. *What a wimp. What a freak. What a loner.* Come on, I'm tired, leave me alone. *How pathetic. How odd. How childish.* Leave me alone, I'm tired. I'm tired. I'm tired. *You broke the one make-or-break moment in your life. How does that feel?* How do you think it feels? *Ariel will meet someone else on this bus and she will marry him. It'll probably be Gio.* Not now. Leave me alone. *Today will be their anniversary. Every year, on this day, Ariel and Gio will kiss on a Greyhound bus. "Mmmmm," Ariel will purr. "You're so brave, Gio. You are my superhero."* You'll be fine. Everything will be okay. Everything will work out, just like my mom says. Things have a way of working themselves out. They do. They do . . .

A MUFFLED MALE VOICE SHAKES ME FROM MY SLUMBER. MY head hurts. My butt is sore. My shirt is sweaty. Someone is speaking into a microphone.

"Ladies and gentleman, we are approaching New York City."

Whoever is talking, I wish he would stop.

"Make sure you have all of your personal belongings before exiting the bus."

That's when it hits me. We are on a bus. The same bus as Ariel.

"Last stop, Port Authority Bus Terminal, New York City."

I have slept through my destiny.

Next to me, Gio stretches his arms and yawns. "Where are we?" he mumbles.

"Almost there."

"That's good," he says, wiping his eyes.

I smack my forehead with the palm of my left hand.

A flash of recognition crosses his face. "Oh, that's right. Your girl . . ."

Then that muffled voice again. "Hold on, passengers, wait till I stop. Hold on, please. Okay. Thank you for riding with Greyhound."

A single-file line forms instantly. A total of twenty-eight, no, wait, twenty-nine people stand between Ariel and me. Ariel is the sixth passenger off the bus. I lean over to watch her disappear and ride off into the sunset, where my dashed dreams go to die.

She doesn't disappear, though. She moves right. She has luggage! Tall, yellow backpacks. I love you tall, yellow backpacks! I could kiss you if you weren't caked with dust and dirt and bacteria and germs. Ariel stands to the side as Brown hair and Blond hair wait for their bags. Brown hair and Blond hair put their hands on their hips; Ariel looks like the morning dew or the mountain dew—something pretty like that.

I thank Ron for driving safely and climb off the bus with Gio. Although I don't have any luggage, I pretend I do—just to see her eyelashes, or smell the red roses which still smell good even after an early morning bus ride.

"Go ahead," Gio says. "Talk to her."

You will be old and wrinkled and alone. If you're lucky, like Edith and Milton, you will sit in a chair all day long. You will tell lame jokes, rip farts, sip Metamucil, nibble on prunes and count down the hours until your next #2/poop/shit/crap/doo-doo.

No, you will live in a tin hut, where you'll drink brown water and eat green hot dogs with your greasy-chinned roommate, Phil, who will be 110 years old by then and won't have enough money to pay rent. And neither will you. Unless you do something. NOW. DO SOMETHING. NOW!

Gio punches me in the kidney. "Doyouneedhelpwithyourbag?" I spit out.

"Ex*cuse* me?" Brown hair says, laughing. "Was that English?"

I throw my hood on. I am invisible.

"Yeah it *was* English," Gio says. "And *that* was English, too."

"It could be a new dialect," suggests Blond hair. "It sounded almost . . . tribal. Perhaps you could translate it for us?"

I am in my room. Alone. My Batman cape is draped over my body as I close my eyes and—

"My man Rene here is simply being the gentleman that he is and asked if he could help anyone with their bags."

Brown hair laughs again. "What are you, his Afro-puffed bodyguard?"

"I'm his friend."

Blond hair points at Gio. "Well then listen here, friend, we've traveled the world on three pairs of underwear, so—"

Brown hair cuts in. "Actually, it was two pairs."

"Right, two pairs. So, *friend,* I think we can handle our bags, thank you *very much.*"

Ariel looks up at me. Into me. Her eyes are hazel. They look like hazelnuts. They look like almonds. They look like honey-roasted peanuts, all sugary and shiny and delicious.

"I've seen you," she breathes.

I inhale. Flowers grow in my heart. Where once there was dirt, now there are flowers. *Tell her that! Tell her that!*

"I—" My throat is swollen. I am choking on cotton balls.

"I'm Ariel."

"I—" This isn't happening. Not now. Not to me.

"You go to Radcliffe High School, right?"

I nod my head because my voice is broken.

"You're a freshman, right?"

I nod my head because my voice is still broken. There's dramatic music coming from an acoustic guitar and a piano. *This is only a movie, a Will Smith movie. Be smooth like him! Say "Hey, girl." SAY IT!*

"What are you doing here?" she asks.

I can't answer her question with my face. I need a voice. I don't have one. Even if I did, the only word I would say is "Phil," and as far as I'm concerned, Phil doesn't exist—especially in Ariel's world.

Gio steps in front of me. "Rene and I are here on business."

Brown hair huffs. "Oh yeah? What *kind* of business?"

"We're in the business of having fun," Gio says. It sounds like something Phil would say because it's corny and lame and untrue. I don't want my relationship with Ariel to start off with a lie.

"We—" My voice is dead. Bloodied. Buried.

"We're here to get away from school," Gio explains. "We're here for fresh air. We're here because parents are suffocating little pests."

"I hear *that,*" says Blond hair.

"But we're also here because we've never been to New York City," Gio says. "And we're dying to explore it."

"Me too!" Ariel shouts.

"Oh, me too, me too," cries Brown hair.

"And me too," cries Blond hair. "This city—sorry, *the* city—is *pulsing* and I *need* to hear its fluttering heart beat."

Blond hair and Brown hair laugh at, not with, Ariel.

Brown hair rolls her eyes. "You're probably dying to see FAO Schwarz and would kill, kill anybody, to catch a glimpse of the spiritual epicenter of the modern world, the one the only . . ."

"Times Square!" cries Blond hair.

"Where only squares go!" Brown hair adds, pointing at Ariel.

Blond hair and Brown hair laugh at, not with, Ariel.

The switch inside me, the one I discovered in defending Mr. Head from Johnny Van Slyke, is flipped on. *SHUT UP YOU EVIL WITCHES. YOU'RE MORE EVIL THAN CINDERELLA'S EVIL STEPSISTERS. I HOPE YOUR SKIN MELTS OFF AND YOUR BONES RUN AWAY WITHOUT YOU.*

Gio must have seen my muscles swelling up because he puts his hands on my shoulders and whispers for me to relax.

Ariel blushes. "You'll have to excuse my older sisters. They're a little, um—"

"LikeNormanandtheSmartypantsatschool!" I bark.

Ariel smiles. Her teeth are a string of white pearls. Her dimpled cheeks are like the heads of turtles, folding inward when she gets shy.

"Exactly," she says. "Like Norman and the Smartypants at school."

Blond hair and Brown hair laugh at, not with, Ariel.

Ariel touches Brown hair on the arm. "Why don't I meet up with you later?"

"Why? What gives?"

"I think I'm going to hang out with them today," Ariel says.

There are green and pink fireworks—watermelon fireworks—exploding above our heads. The watermelon fireworks drip watermelon onto Ariel's red hair. I think of licking the nectar off her hair, but then I remember that this isn't a fantasy. Ariel said she wants to be with me! Run away with me! Marry me on a mountain!

"It's only for the day," Ariel tells her evil sisters. "I'll give you a call later."

Brown hair shrugs. "Fine with us. You frolic around with your little high school friends and give us a call when you're hungry."

Brown hair and Blond hair throw their bags over their shoulders and scurry away.

"Talk to you later." Ariel waves, then faces us.

Or is it only me she's facing?

At Port Authority Bus Terminal there are lines everywhere. Lines and buses and water fountains that taste like metal and snack shops with microwavable cheeseburgers and bathrooms that only make you dirtier. If Ariel wasn't here, I would turn back and go home.

"I'm Gio, this is Rene. He just woke up, so he's not very talkative right now. Not a morning person, you know?"

In front of a dirty bathroom, an unfunny play unfolds before my eyes:

Ariel: "I'm not a morning person, either. Sorry about my sisters."

Gio: "No sweat. Glad to have the company."

Ariel: "Where do you guys want to go?"

Gio: "Wherever you want to go."

Ariel: "I wouldn't know where to start."

Gio: "It's not like we have plans or anything."

Ariel: "Me neither."

Gio: "Are you hungry?"

Ariel: "Starving. You know what I'm in the mood for?"

Gio: "Let me guess: pretzels, anything from a street vendor."

Ariel: "Exactly! Anything they don't sell back home in the south Jersey malls."

Gio: "From someone you don't *see* back home in the south Jersey malls."

Ariel: "Exactly!"

[Their eyes meet. Watermelon fireworks explode over their shoulders.]

I want to separate them, tear them apart, but I don't know how. Separating people's eyes isn't like tearing magnets off a refrigerator. I mean, it's not like I can pull their eyeballs out. That's illegal and immoral and, not to sound shallow or anything, I wouldn't marry Ariel if she didn't have eyes.

On second thought, if she didn't have eyes, it would be like being in a dark classroom. I would be a social butterfly.

Gio turns to me. "Cool with you, brother man?" he asks.

Sure, it's totally cool that you're stealing my wife. I don't know how to tell Gio that I no longer want him to be my friar, so I say, "Yeah, I see how it is." As soon as the words leave my mouth, they repeat themselves in my head like a broken record: *Yeah, I see how it is. Yeah, I see how it is. Yeah, I see how it is.*

Gio touches my arm and asks if I'm all right.

I nod. *Yeah, I see how it is.* I see how it is.

"Well then, shall we?" Gio asks, pointing to the stairwell.

"Maybe we should wait out the rain," Ariel suggests. "Everyone else is waiting."

"But we're in New York City," Gio says, grabbing Ariel, *my* Ariel, by the hand. She smiles. Wedding bells bang against my eardrums.

"Come on, Ariel. I'll count down from three."

Ariel giggles like a bride about to toss her bouquet.

"Three, two, one . . . go!"

They sprint up the stairs, hand in hand, laughing in the rain. I see how it is, but I follow anyway.

Outside, the wind snaps umbrellas in half: limp pieces of fabric hang over broken limbs like burial shrouds, like folding parachutes, like my ice cream wedding cake melting into spilled milk. And it's all Gio's fault.

It's raining so hard that within seconds my gray sweatshirt is a wet sponge, but Ariel's purple sweater doesn't even look wet. I guess that's part of her Angel powers. Gio wouldn't know anything about that. Or would he?

A homeless man shivers on the sidewalk, holding a small paper cup of coins filled up halfway with rain. Ariel digs into her pocket and drops a quarter into his cocktail.

"Yo, brother man, you want a strong umbrella!" Gio shouts through the wind.

To avoid talking to Gio, I pretend I am *so* overwhelmed by New York City that I lost my hearing. I spin in place with my mouth propped open from shock.

"Yo, what gives?"

I keep spinning. "Look at all these skyscrapers. How tall they are! Look at these lights. How bright they are!"

"Rene. Yo, Rene."

"Look at how many people there are. How wonderful!"

"Yo, brother man, wait with Ariel for a sec, all right?"

I stop spinning. "Nice of you to share her," I say instead of think.

"What'd you just say?"

"Wow, look at these television screens. You can see every little detail!"

"I'll be right back, Rene. Yo, wait with her." Gio hops over puddles and skips through crowds, dashing through the rain like a superhero—a lying, cheating, stealing superhero.

I look over at Ariel. She's spinning, too.

"We're spinning together," I whisper.

She ignores me.

I tap her on the shoulder so that I can touch her. Her sweater is a velvety cloud.

"Oh, Rene," she says, blushing. "It's so easy to just . . . space out." Rain drips down her perfect face. "Isn't the city *amazing*?"

"I—"

"The lights and the buildings and the people. Even in the rain, it's so alive."

"I—"

"Get under," Gio says.

Grinning, he holds a new umbrella, a gold umbrella, big enough for a family of four. It probably belonged to a family of four a minute ago.

"Who *are* you?" Ariel squeals, leaping under the umbrella.

"I'm Rainman." Gio elbows me. "Right, Rene?"

I stare at my shoelaces. They are wet, which means they are now dark gray instead of light gray. "Rene, are you coming?" With each passing second, my shoelaces are getting darker and dirtier, and soon they'll be *so* dark and dirty that—

"Don't be silly, Rene. You'll get sick standing out in the rain." Ariel says this. So I obey.

At the first corner, Ariel and Gio walk up to a street vendor. Gio asks me if I want a hot dog or a pretzel. I pretend that I am deaf.

"Greetings, pretzel man," Gio says, licking his lips. "Two hot dogs. You know what, make that three hot dogs. And two pretzels."

"Breakfast," the vendor says, pointing to a row of bagels and muffins. "Only breakfast."

"What?" Gio whines. "But we traveled so far for your pretzels, pretzel man."

"Journey back this way in three hours," he grunts. "For now, breakfast."

Ariel laughs. "It's fine," she says. "I'll have a bagel. With cream cheese. And jelly."

Gio sighs. "Same for me, I guess. Actually, make that two more." Gio turns to me. "For when you get hungry."

"I won't *get* hungry," I mutter.

Halfway down the block, Ariel pulls off a piece of bagel, places it daintily into her mouth. As she reaches for another piece, a wad of grape jelly falls onto her sweater. She wipes it off with a napkin like nothing happened. Of course she does. Then she heads back to the street vendor for a few more napkins.

"You want to take a hike, Rene?" Gio asks.

He wants me to take a hike, a really long hike, so that Gio can kiss Ariel until the sun sets and he proposes with a plastic ring that she'll love, of course, because she's a humble Angel, but he is mean and shallow and cruel and not my friend. I wish I would have never fallen in that stupid brown puddle last week in school. Jesus H. Christ, why would Gio say that to me? Forget Gio. There's not even an *H.* in Jesus' name. That's how stupid Gio is. I'm better off without him. Much better off. I'm glad this happened because now I know what kind of man Gio is. He is a mean and shallow and cruel man. Why don't *you* take a hike? Take a hike with Phil! Go to China with him. Rent a cabin in the woods and grow old together, *so* old that you rip bare-butted farts all over each other on the way to the bathroom. And neither one of you will ever write to me again!

"Yo, brother man, you all right?"

"I'm not your brother and you're not a man. Men don't steal each other's wives."

"What are you *talking* about?"

"I'm not stupid."

"I never said you were."

My voice is shaking. "Actions speak loud. I mean, they speak . . . Actions speak louder than words."

"What did I say, Rene? What did I do?"

"You . . . and . . . with . . . Ariel. You told me to take a hike."

He takes a deep breath. "Rene, I swear on my mother's life and on our friendship, that I would never steal Ariel. I swear to you, friend, that my intentions are innocent. You have nothing to worry about, I promise you that."

"But the hike . . ."

"I meant that *we* should take a hike. *We* should go for a walk. Explore. Get to know the city."

Ariel skips back toward us, napkins in hand.

Gio turns to me and whispers, "So are we cool, brother man?"

Because Ariel is close enough to hear me, I say, "Of course we're cool. Where to?"

Gio suggests that the first order of business should be to find places that honor student discounts, but before long I realize that student discounts are like Phil's love: rumored to be constant, advertised through word of mouth, but offered only in strange times and places. Take, for instance, the movie theater. Student discounts are accepted during the week before 7:00 p.m. only on days that aren't holidays. Even though we're the only ones here during the week before 7:00 p.m. on a non-holiday, the ticket lady says it's "a holiday week," whatever *that* means.

Gio has two hundred dollars for the next few days, including money for wherever the hell we plan on sleeping, so a ten-dollar movie is out of the picture. Get it? Out of the *picture*. Sometimes, and I never know when or why it happens, there's something funny in my head and it doesn't leave until my cheeks are sore. The out-of-the-picture joke is what's funny in my head right now, but because it's not *that* funny, it stays there for only a few minutes.

Anyway, even though we're in New York City, and even though it's already pretty dark outside because of the rain, I want the sun to set. Why? I already told you: nobody makes out in the daytime; people kiss only at night. Why? It's simple: during the daytime, people can see you.

I'm not an artsy person, but the Museum of Modern Art (MoMA) gives me hope.

It's a quiet place, so nobody notices that Ariel has stolen my voice. Nobody yells at me or tells me what I have to say is stupid or obvious or crazy. The people who *do* talk in museums might as well write the word "Smartypants" on a nametag and stick it on their back. Since neither Gio nor Ariel is a Smartypants, we are silent for 129 minutes.

I'm especially hopeful at MoMA because plain blue pictures and green polka-dot paintings and solid black posters are valued and loved. One Smartypants sticks his face really close to an all-red picture and whispers, "Magnificent genius." When I was in elementary school, Phil never said *my* art projects were magnificent *or* genius; he just trashed them when I wasn't looking. I know it was him because I used to spy on him from the next room with camouflage binoculars.

Even though MoMA makes me think of Phil, it is my favorite museum ever and I want to stay here another few hours and maybe even sleep over if we have no other place to crash tonight, but Ariel wants to get some air so I tell her what a great idea that is.

The weather has cleared up. The sun isn't out but at least it stopped raining. The sidewalk outside the museum is still wet, but that doesn't stop a whole flock of pigeons from congregating there. There must be two hundred of them. Obviously, I want to chase after them and yell "Rarrrrr" like I used to do when Phil took me to the zoo, but I don't, for obvious reasons. Gio is not as prudent. He runs after them and swings and jabs with his leg, trying to kick as many defenseless pretty pigeons as he can until I roar, "WHAT ARE YOU DOING?"

Gio's leg stops in mid-kick.

"Well, look who decided to wake up . . ." he says. "And it's pigeons—*pigeons*—that wake you from your slumber."

I want to wake you from your slumber when I turn, no put, *no* punch *your lights out.* I don't say this because it's a terrible comeback.

"You act like pigeons are your favorite animal," he says, laughing.

"WHAT IF THEY ARE?!" I thunder back, which is a terrible idea. Just what Ariel wants in a future husband: a love of dirty birds that flutter around, pooping out wet, white paint on people's heads. Ariel's too pretty for pigeons. She deserves flamingos or parrots or, better yet, peacocks. Since peacocks, flamingos, and parrots don't marry or fraternize or make out with ugly pigeons, I suck in air through my mouth so that I can take my words back.

"I think that's sweet," she says. "I like pigeons, too."

I exhale. "I think it's b'noodles that you like pigeons."

She laughs. "What does *that* mean?"

I throw a look over to Gio for permission to plagiarize. He nods.

"B'noodles means uniquely cool," I explain. "I made it up because b'noodles is uniquely cool and fun to say."

"That's genius," she says. "Pure genius."

Maybe things *will* work out after all. Since Ariel and I both like pigeons, maybe someday we can capture a pigeon and keep it as a pet. We'll keep it in a cage, of course—nothing crazy. In the afternoons, after I come home from a long day of writing at the office, I'll say hello to our pigeon and pet his gray body and purple and green neck, and tell him (our pigeon will be a guy) that he's good-looking and smart and will someday grow up to be a social butterfly like his mommy (Ariel).

And someday, Ariel and I will have a child who will be so smart that by the age of three, he or she will say, "My mommy isn't the pigeon's mommy! The pigeon's mommy is a pigeon!"

Maybe we'll even open a pet store and—

Ariel's phone rings. Her sisters tell her that she must be ready to leave at 10:00 p.m., and that they'll call her back then with directions.

Oh, and her sisters are staying at a friend's house. They made friends already. I've only made one friend in fourteen years, but I can't waste time thinking about it and thinking about it because it's 1:00 p.m. which means that it's lunchtime and that I have nine more hours to propose to Ariel. We pass a Wendy's. I don't want to be too obvious about proposing, so I keep walking and don't say anything. I write a note in my brain to go back later after I know how to get to the beach.

Gio suggests we revisit the street vendor who only served breakfast during breakfast time. Ariel agrees.

Later tonight, after Ariel and I are married, we won't have to go along with Gio's stupid, unfunny plans. I mean, leave the street vendor alone! What did he ever do to Gio besides wake up at the buttcrack of dawn, put on his chef hat, and bake bagels in the middle of the street?

THE STREET VENDOR IS AT THE SAME CORNER WHERE WE left him. The only difference is that he has a new cart. He doesn't look very happy to see us.

"Good day, pretzel man," Gio says, bowing at the waist. "Your bagels were scrumptious and satisfying, but after conquering your city our bellies are in need of more nourishment. As promised, we have journeyed back to you for your lunch delicacies."

"Yippee ki-yay," the vendor mumbles. "Will you accept a flock of sheep as a sign of my deep gratitude?"

Gio gasps. "Pretzel man, what has gotten into you? You sold us bagels with cream cheese and jelly just a few hours ago. You *really* don't remember us?"

"Oh. Yes." The vendor yawns. "How could I forget?"

"Just gimme three pretzels and three hot dogs," Gio mutters.

"With mustard?"

"Whatever."

The man hands over the food. "If you journey back for dinner in five hours, I will have my goats and sheep waiting for you." He laughs wildly at his own joke. At least I think it's a joke.

We take our lunch delicacies to a small, wobbly table on a pedestrian-only street in the middle of Times Square. Ariel tears off small pieces of her pretzel; Gio chomps into his like a wild tiger; I don't eat my pretzel because a guy handing out flyers for a comedy club just came up to our table and said, "You guys like comedy?" I said, "Yeah" because I love jokes, but the guy didn't even hear me because he had already started to say, "I see a budding romance in front of me." He was talking about Gio and Ariel. "If you come to the comedy club," he said, "you could pee your pants, which is terrible for a date but good for the soul, so I recommend bringing a change of underwear."

Gio told him to get lost but I'm worried that we still may wind up going to that stupid comedy club. I really hope we don't because I don't want Gio and Ariel's romance to bud like an orange flower or Angel flower and I don't want to laugh so hard that I pee my pants because I don't have a change of underwear.

Ariel and Gio are talking about how wild and free New

York City is but I can't focus on what they're saying because the bright lights of Times Square burn my eyes and sitcoms play on buildings and sports headlines snake across the tops of restaurants and people hand money to a guy in a Statue of Liberty costume to escort them onto the top floor of a naked bus. There aren't any bugs in the air but there are pigeons everywhere and nobody seems to notice because a naked cowboy plays his guitar in the middle of the street and a guy spray-painted in gold stands on a platform and pretends to be a frozen superhero. Almost two hours have gone by and the fake superhero hasn't even blinked but Ariel has because she bats her eyelashes at Gio, who doesn't seem to notice because he, too, watches the naked cowboy play his guitar in the middle of the street while the guy spray-painted in gold stands on a platform and pretends to be a frozen superhero.

I want to write all this down but it's all happening so fast and I don't have a pen or a notebook or even a receipt because street vendors don't give receipts and nobody would believe me anyway if I wrote that the New Year's Eve crystal ball hangs above a steaming hot bowl of Cup of Noodles, or that people hand twenty dollars to a stranger to draw a picture of their big nose and greasy chin, or that the policemen with dogs sniff for drugs instead of runaway children like me, or that taxis crash into one another and *then* honk, or that people with cameras the size of a baby elephant take pictures of other people with cameras the size of a baby elephant, or that a line of middle-aged men and women snake around and around and around the letters TKTS, or that kids wearing cardboard boxes hand out coupons for 15 percent off a haircut, or that billboards advertise beer bottles in high definition, or that women snuggle up to the naked cowboy as people with cameras the size of a baby elephant snap at least ten shots just in case somebody blinked.

And Ms. Adelman thinks *I* need therapy . . .

At the end of our long lunch, Ariel suggests seeing a Broadway show but Gio and I don't have a ton of money left, so we walk to the only free place in the entire city, Central Park, which isn't *really* free because you get hungry walking around in nature and there are as many pretzel men as there are pretty green trees. Every half a mile, Gio says hello to a pretzel man and tells him about our journey and buys three hot dogs and three pretzels and soon we've spent over twenty dollars but at least we're in nature and Ariel looks beautiful in the reflection of a pond with lily pads and moss and ducks.

Ariel rips off pieces of her pretzel and tosses them into the pond for the ducks to eat for lunch. She tries to aim her pretzel pieces at the baby ducks, but the big ugly ducks with the puffy feathers and sharp beaks keep stealing them. "Get out of the way," she cries, "let the little guy have a turn." I hope she feels the same way about spending time with me, the little guy, instead of with Gio, and I think of proposing right here, right now, but Gio is too close and so are the packs of sweaty runners huffing and puffing along the runners' path in short shorts, showing everyone their hairy legs.

I'm glad Phil isn't here. If he were, I would rip out all the hair on his chest and legs, but that would scare Ariel so maybe I would just run away or dive into the pond and swim around with the baby ducks and hope the big ducks wouldn't bite my head off.

We keep walking around and around the park and we pass the zoo but we don't go in because we don't have money and I don't want to think of orangutans and Phil any more than I already am and before we know it, it's 6:00 p.m. and the sky is purple and pink and it's time for dinner. Gio wants to return to his favorite street vendor but Ariel says she wants to eat sushi because they don't have sushi restaurants back home. I once heard an evil, frightening rumor that sushi is actually raw fish, but Johnny Van Slyke's friend, Norman, told me that so it must not be true.

It's true. "Sushi contains raw ingredients." It says that on the front of the menu for Yuki Sushi, a very stupid name for a restaurant. Why would you want your customers to know that the food is yucky? That's like opening a Batman store and calling it Boring, Lame-o Batman Store.

Yuki Sushi's picture frames are filled with a panda, a butterfly, a sitting Buddha, a lying-down Buddha, and a standing Buddha. On top of my plate are chopsticks, which will be helpful in case I really *did* get lice from the outside of Gio's house or from walking around in Central Park. There's no nurse in the restaurant, so I'll have to pick the lice out myself. My ping-pong paddles trade a few shots—*I don't have lice.* Yes you do. *No I don't.* Yes you do.—until Ariel says, "Rene, Gio, honestly, why aren't you guys in school today?"

Gio puts his elbows on the table. "Do you want the *real* answer or the let's-pretend-you're-dumb-and-I'm-dumb-so-therefore-I'll-smile-and-pretend-everything-is-gravy type of answer?" he asks.

"Which one do you think?" Ariel mocks.

"The let's-pretend-you're-dumb-and-I'm-dumb-so-therefore-I'll-smile-and-pretend-everything-is-gravy type of answer?"

"Seriously," she says. "Tell me."

I don't have lice. Yes you do. They're so big and disgusting that Ariel will see and smell them on the beach. *That's not true.* Save a pair of chopsticks. *Shut UP! I won't need them. There aren't any lice in my hair. There aren't any lice in my hair. There aren't any lice in my hair.*

"In that case, Rene, why don't you tell her," Gio says, nodding in Ariel's direction.

"I don't have lice," I say, to set the record straight.

He chuckles. "Not about lice, about why we're here."

"Oh, well, Phil—he—was—Phil." My voice breaks again.

Gio turns to Ariel. "What he means to say is that his dad's a lowlife, like mine. But unlike mine, Rene's dad came back. Since Rene needed a place to sleep, we . . ."

I grab a napkin and tear at its edges until I have three small pieces and one big piece. I roll the three small pieces into tiny balls and curve the one larger piece into a horseshoe. I put them on the table and align my smiley face.

"But where are you gonna sleep tonight?" Ariel asks.

Gio coughs into his hand. "Where there's a will, there's a way."

"You're gonna need more than a will," she says. "How about money? Skipping school to go to New York City without a place to stay . . . You gotta be responsible."

"Look at *you*," Gio says, getting defensive. "Tell me, how are you any different from us?"

"I'm—well, I guess I'm not," she says. "I just have a better cover."

"Your sisters."

Ariel nods. "My mom trusts them, so she let me come along. It's a present for . . . " Angels don't like to brag, especially the Angel of Angels, but she needs to explain herself so she does: "It's a present for doing well last year."

"Doing *well*? You mean you passed most of your classes?"

"I was at the top of my class."

"Alphabetically? Like 'A' for 'Ariel'?"

"I get As. All As. I was the valedictorian of my eighth-grade class."

"Which makes you want to run away . . . Why?"

I've heard this before so I know what to say. I clear my throat and speak from memory: "Life can be so stressful and overwhelming, so overwhelming that it feels like you're drowning, so sometimes you need a break, to come up for air."

Ariel smiles. "You truly have insight, Rene, you truly do."

"The gentleman pays for meals," Gio says. "And since I'm a gentleman, I'll pay." I, too, am a gentleman, but Ariel already knows it so I don't have to say it. Show, don't tell, you know?

When the bill comes, I sneak a peek: $42.67, plus tip. Gio must be running out of money but he doesn't say anything about it. Maybe he has a wad of fresh bills stashed in his socks or in his underwear or under a mattress, like they do in the movies.

I finger a quarter in my pocket and as I get up from the table, that quarter falls out of my hand and rolls onto the floor. George Washington is looking down, so I don't pick it up. But the waiter does.

"You dropped a quarter, sir," he says.

I shake my head furiously.

"I think you dropped this, sir," he says. "It fell out of your pocket."

"No, it didn't," I tell him.

"I'm pretty sure it did, sir."

"IT DID NOT!" I shout, and run out the door. It's dark outside, which makes me feel better for obvious reasons.

A block away from the restaurant, two homeless men cover their bodies with wool blankets. Ariel reaches into her pocket; Gio and I are copycats. The homeless men get three dollars apiece.

With two hours until Ariel's curfew and a Wendy's right down the street, the timing is perfect. She knows I'm a gentleman. She thinks I'm sweet. Right on schedule—until Gio shows Ariel his "Gray Suburbia" poem and begs her to join him and Rene at a New York City nightclub.

"I hear what you're saying," Ariel says. "I do, I really do, but where are we going to get fake ID's from? Besides, the penalty is pretty steep for using them."

"But we gotta do something," Gio protests. "The clock is melting away. Soon the hourglass will be empty."

I step forward with a genius idea. "Why don't we get fake mustaches?"

Gio gives me a high five. "You really *do* have insight, brother man."

Ariel shakes her head in disbelief. "No offense or anything, but that doesn't make much sense," she says. "I mean, I'm not going to wear one and Gio doesn't even need one. He already has a mustache *and* a beard."

Gio strokes his goatee. "You speak the truth. My hair could be the answer to this pickle jam," he says. "But there's no penalty for wearing a fake mustache, and there's someone among us who could use a little bit more hair on his face."

THE DOLLAR STORE SELLS AN "INCOGNITO PACKAGE": A black, furry mustache, a beige plastic nose, and black glasses for five dollars, which isn't *one* dollar like the store advertises (what's with this city?).

Gio tells us, "It's like taking an umbrella from a baby" and buys three. We rip open the package and try them on as soon as we leave the store. Ariel looks beautiful even with a bushy mustache. I don't look as beautiful, but I can't stop laughing.

Gio puts on an especially serious face and says, "Now, you gotta look serious when you walk up to the bouncer, or else we have no shot of getting in."

"How will we know which one is the bouncer?" I ask.

"Don't worry, you'll know," he says. "The bouncer will be the big guy looking to bounce people's heads on the sidewalk."

Even if he's joking, I don't think I can go through with this. My mom used to say, "If your friends jumped from the Brooklyn Bridge, would you jump, too?" I would respond that I didn't have any friends. "But if you did . . ." she would insist, to which I would say, "I wouldn't jump from the Brooklyn Bridge, but I might consider another one." The joke isn't funny anymore because Gio's jumping off the Brooklyn Bridge, and I am jumping, too. It's a stupid plan, but I'm not doing it for him; I'm doing it for Ariel, for whom I would run around naked in the dead of winter in a forest full of wild, rabid dogs with gallons of poisonous saliva in their mouths—all for a peck on the cheek.

The bouncer outside of Metro has muscles the size of Antarctica. He doesn't strip me or search me or bounce me upside down on the sidewalk; he simply sticks out his arm, palm up, like a crossing guard. Then he tells us to take a hike.

So does the bouncer at Crystal.

Dejected, we walk into a dirty alley, where Ariel and I rip off our disguises.

"We're not going out like this!" Gio insists. "Not like this. Not without trying."

"It's okay," Ariel says. "There'll be other times. If it's not meant to be, it's not meant to be."

She believes in destiny! I believe in destiny! We have something in common. Maybe, just maybe, oh please, please let it be: we may share a *common destiny*?

"I'll be back," Gio mutters. "Let me talk to one of the bouncers by myself . . . see if I can work my magic."

In the meantime, I hope that Ariel and I will make out. We are alone, and it's extremely dark outside, which means that it is appropriate and legal to kiss like a pair of wild dogs that aren't allergic to each other.

Her rosy lips and rosy cheeks match the color of her hair. She has seven tiny freckles, four on her left cheek and three on her right. They look like the Milky Way, but I can't tell if they line up *exactly* like the Milky Way because it's 9:18, and it's too dark to see.

Despite the torturous desire setting our bodies aflame, we must keep our emotions locked in a vault buried deep within our chests—at least until Gio completes his mission. Gio's been gone for 168 seconds. My left hand smells like soy sauce and raw fish.

I wish I had binoculars—camouflaged ones, of course. With squinted eyes, I follow Gio as he approaches the entrance to Fantasy, where two bouncers cross their arms against their large chests. Next to the bouncers are three television screens. Gio is on one of the TVs!

They know! They know everything. They know he is a minor. That's why he's on TV. Maybe he's on *America's Most Wanted*! How do they know so quickly? What has he done to deserve all the media attention?

That's it! The umbrellas! They must have had a warrant out for his arrest for years. Or maybe it's the search party. Maybe they think Gio kidnapped me.

This is it. This is doomsday!

Where are the cops? Why are they waiting so long to arrest him? Why wouldn't they spring like leopards and dig their nails into him?

It must be a sting attack, an undercover operation. No, Gio, no! Don't walk up to the bouncers. They're really cops. Don't reach into your wallet. Don't give them identification. Don't pay them off. That will only mean a darker doomsday.

"You okay, Rene?" Ariel asks, touching my right shoulder. "You look tense."

And *you* look a little too relaxed and beautiful to be sent to prison for life if Gio rats us out, which he'll do in order to reach a plea bargain, which is what hardened criminals like Gio do on television, but if he truly *is* one of America's most wanted, he won't be able to reach a plea bargain because truly slimy slimeballs don't get a second chance to live a clean life.

Gio shakes hands with one of the bouncers and walks

back to us, grinning like a clown, which is a good sign, but two men slam their car doors shut and walk toward Gio, which is a bad sign, a *very* bad sign. One of them is wearing sunglasses, which is another bad sign, because everyone knows that Feds wear sunglasses even when it's dark outside.

"NOOOOOOOOOOOOOOOOOOOOOOOOOOOO!"

That's what my brain shouts but my mouth doesn't shout anything because I don't want to compromise Ariel. She is a top priority. Her contribution to this mission must remain classified.

The man with glasses nods at Gio, yet another bad sign, but the other man doesn't even look at him.

Gio makes it across the street without being gagged and cuffed and thrown into the back of an unmarked van, which is a good sign.

I tug his arm until we are at the other end of the alley.

"Okay, Rene, *okay*. Let go of me. *Jesus!*"

I don't want to tell Gio about the sting operation until I'm sure that it's real. The last thing I want to do is worry Ariel.

"There's no alcohol at this club, so you only have to be eighteen to get in," Gio says. "I don't know how you guys feel about a club with no liquor, but it doesn't bother me: I'd rather not become a drunk like my old man."

"But we're not eight—" I start.

"I know. I know. We're not eighteen. But trust me; I got it taken care of. I slipped the bouncer forty bucks to let in my two 'cousins'"—he flexes his index and middle fingers—"who are visiting for the day. So as long as my 'cousins' don't have high squeaky voices or wear Batman capes or anything like that, he'll let you in."

This worries me for obvious reasons.

On the way to the club, I keep my head down and try not to step on any cracks. I avoid most of them, but I accidentally step on two cracks, so I look over to Gio and Ariel to see if they noticed. I am glad they didn't because that way they won't blame me if we don't get in the club.

Right before we approach the bouncer, I check my watch. It's 9:22, and 9+2+2=13, so I tell Gio and Ariel to please wait. I bend down to tie my shoe, and while I'm down there, I spot a nickel with Thomas Jefferson's face on top, so I scoop it into my hand and check my watch. It's 9:23, so I stand up.

"Well, here are my cousins," Gio tells the bouncer. "Fine people, but they don't turn eighteen for another month. Young 'uns . . ." The bouncer is a big man, a very big man, but he's also a very lenient man.

Inside, the lights are flickering on and off, on and off, as if Johnny Van Slyke were the DJ and this were Mr. Head's room.

It's not. Not at all.

Guys in sleeveless shirts rub against girls in tank tops. Lights blink like electrocuted fireflies. Arms move at superhuman speed. I know it's a dance floor but I can't see the floor. Bodies crash into one another, bouncing to beats that pound my brain until my head splits and I have two heads and two headaches. I want to throw up, which would be doomsday, especially because Gio is already out on the dance floor grinding with two girls, one in front of him and one behind him. They're having a Gio sandwich. If I throw up or if my splitting brain oozes onto the floor, nobody will be there to look after Ariel, who is smiling nervously. Her dimples are larger than usual, which means that her cheeks must really be scared . . . like me.

I don't even want to be near Ariel because I don't know what to do with my hands or arms or legs or back or feet, but everybody else seems to know what to do with them, which means that either they took years of dancing lessons or I'm a bumbling oaf with two brains.

I still have part of my brain left. I know this because my Batman watch says that it's 9:52. I have eight minutes left to propose, and I remember that I need to do it on a beach, so when Ariel isn't looking directly at me, I ask a brown-haired girl with six nose rings if she knows which way the beach is. She looks me up and down and laughs. Since she must be on drugs—why else would she stick that many rings through her booger-filled nose?—I ask a tall, muscular guy wearing a backward baseball hat if *he* knows which way the beach is. "The beach," he says, flexing his right bicep, "is that way." I thank him profusely, but then I understand his joke: he's making fun of my muscles. He punches my right arm—hard. Ariel doesn't see this because she's watching Gio, which I don't mind interrupting, so I tell her that she only has seven minutes left until her evil sisters kidnap her and her carriage turns into a pumpkin—or something like that.

I don't think she understands me, because she points to her right ear and yells, "WHAT?! I CAN'T HEAR YOU!"

"I said, 'We don't have much time left.'"

"I CAN'T HEAR YOU! SHOUT IN MY EAR!"

I don't want to shout in her ear because that would give her an earache, which can be as painful as a headache, but I've never been that close to her before, so maybe I—wait, wait, why is she leaning so close to me? Oh, God. Oh, Jesus H. Christ. This is it!

"DO YOU WANT TO DANCE?" she shouts in my ear.

There is a better chance of me rolling around in cat fur than dancing to scary music with scary people in scary lighting who stare at me as I try but fail to dance, but Ariel grabs me by the arm and pulls me on the dance floor.

Do-you-think-you're-bet-ter-off-a-lone? The music buzzes through my brain. *Do-you-think-you're-bet-ter-off-a-lone?*

Ariel looks even prettier with the lights flashing and disappearing. *Do-you-think-you're-bet-ter-off-a-lone?* This is a movie, I tell myself, when Ariel's eyes flicker like lightning. *Do-you-think-you're-bet-ter-off-a-lone?* It's a dramatic and embarrassing movie, I tell myself, as Ariel shakes my arms as if I am a doll on a string and she is a puppet master. *I-wanna-get-close-in-this-club . . . In-this-club . . . In-this-club . . .* It's a funny movie, I tell myself, as Ariel laughs at my wiggling arms and legs that look like a fish out of water. It's an action movie, I tell myself, as a guy bumps into me and yells "Yo, watch where you at!" It's a movie with a happy, feel-good ending with watermelon fireworks: the kind that delivers moments of clarity and peace and understanding, I tell myself, as she rushes in to hug me awkwardly but beautifully and brushes her lips on my right cheek, which I will never, ever—not in a million, billion, trillion years—wash again.

"Sorry," she says.

I know exactly what to say: Don't be sorry. It's okay to love me. It's okay to marry me. *I-wanna-get-close-in-this-club . . . In-this-club . . . In-this-club.* It's okay to accept that we are one. *In-this-club* . . . that your sisters are part of a past life . . . *In-this-club* . . . that you are Juliet and I am Romeo . . . *In-this-club* . . . that the Capulets and the Montagues are simply strange families with strange names . . . *In-this-club* . . . that we are in the East, and you are the sun . . . *In-this-club* . . . that you will never have to say, "Oh Rene, Rene! Where art thou, Rene?" because I know that I'm *not* better off alone; I am better off here. In this club. In love. With you.

"Sorry about that," Ariel says, out of breath. "Some big, rude guy bumped into me from behind. I hope I didn't step on your foot."

"HICKORY, DICKORY, DOCK, THE MOUSE RAN UP THE CLOCK. The clock struck one . . . Lunch!"

I keep telling myself this joke in order to make myself feel better because the clock has struck ten and the beach is at least an hour away. Besides, Ariel didn't even kiss me; she bumped into me. Then she got the phone call from her sisters.

Now she's hugging Gio goodbye. She lingers there for too long. The DJ scratches his record and the songs repeat. *Do-you-think-you're-bet-ter-off-a-lone? Do you think you're better off alone?* Ariel agrees to let me walk her to the taxi. At the very least, I want her to remember me as a gentleman.

It's gotten cold outside. I can see my breath when I breathe out of my mouth *and* nose. When you can see your nose breath, you know it's so cold that you need an Eskimo jacket. I don't have an Eskimo jacket—I don't even have a light jacket—but I have a hooded sweatshirt. I offer it to her. She shakes her head. She doesn't even say "No, thank you." Maybe she's not really an Angel.

Ariel waves for a taxi. She can't stand another second with me alone.

"Goodbye, Rene," she says, hugging me. No, it's not even a hug; it's more like a pat on the back, the kind you get from a baseball coach after losing a meaningless game.

I know I have one last chance to confess my love. I know I will only be young once, and that someday all I will have left is the black-and-white photo album of my memories—of what I did when I still could.

But I'm not even here anymore, watching her open the taxi door and file in. I'm already looking through my photo album and pleading to God to give me one more chance to do it over; to open my mouth and toss my guts onto the concrete and tell her what we should do, what we *must* do if we are ever going to survive in this dark, cruel world.

The taxi drives off.

By the time I turn around to face the club, Gio is on his way out. He has two shades of red lipstick on his cheeks.

"Got digits!" he shouts. "Let me show you."

I muster a weak smile.

Gio reaches into his right pocket for the numbers. Then his left pocket, and then his back pocket.

"You lost the numbers *already*?" I snarl. His happiness must disappear. He must come down to earth and feel as dirty and stupid as me. "I can't believe you lost them already!"

"The numbers . . . I wrote them on my hands," he stammers.

"Then what was in your pockets?"

I already know the answer before he says it. I turn around and picture Ariel climbing into her yellow taxi. She waves at me this time. I follow the taxi with my eyes as it starts down the street. Ariel is waving from the back window. Tears spill down her cheeks. She blows me a kiss. I blow her one back. The taxi stops. She runs out, beaming. "Yes! Yes!" she shouts, wiping her tears and snot on her sleeve. "I do! I do!" Her red hair bounces with each step as—

"We have no money," Gio says.

"I COULD SELL MY WATCH. OR MY SNEAKERS. OR MY BODY. I could sell *something,*" Gio pleads, twirling his hair. "I could clean windshields. Or do magic tricks. I could beg."

We pass a Wendy's on the left-hand side.

"We could hitchhike home," Gio continues. "I mean, I know there are urban legends and horror movies about guys being dumped on the side of the road without their heads, but it's worth a shot."

I wonder if Ariel made a bet with her sisters that she could survive the day with me. If she won the bet, I hope the money spoils her and makes her a rotten apple.

"We could steal bikes or skateboards or something like that and grab onto the back of a truck like in *Back to the Future* and ride all the way home."

Gio and I step over two homeless guys lying on the street. I am careful not to touch them because they might be my new neighbors.

"We could sleep in the movie theater or something. No, never mind. Tried that with a girl last year. Damn flashlights."

I should've slept at Gio's house. I could've cracked a

window and stuck my head out to avoid Rufus's poisonous saliva. The bathtub was an option. Animals never go in the bathroom. I should've slept in his bathtub.

"I could call the girls I met at the club. On second thought, scratch that." He stares hopelessly at his palms. "I must have been sweating like your dad, I mean, your Phil. The ink must have run. I can't read any of these numbers."

Even though Mr. Head's desk was cold and lonely, I would pay my life savings to be there now.

"We could call our parents. No, scratch that. My mom would ground me for the next 150 years, not that she even cares. But she would still ground me, just to prove to my sister that she's in control and can be a disciplinarian when she wants to. I'm not going down like that."

Why did we have to buy sushi? And drinks? Ariel could have paid for *something.* And why did Gio have to bribe that stupid bouncer?

"There are probably hostels around here somewhere if we can somehow raise twenty dollars. I know you don't want to beg for money but . . ."

Before this moment, I had no idea what the hell a pickle jam was. It's a good thing that Gio, the master of escaping pickle jams, is here.

"I'm sorry, Rene. I'm so sorry. I can't think of anything else, can you?"

The street is wet from all the rain in the afternoon. There are brown puddles on the ground that look like the one in which Gio and I met. I wish he had left me there.

Gio grabs a Styrofoam cup blowing in the wind, and then hands me a piece of cardboard caked in dirt. I want to wash my hands but there aren't any bathrooms around. "If we can find a marker, this might help," he says.

We don't find a marker, but we find a blue pen. We sit down on the sidewalk. It feels like glass. Gio writes on the cardboard, "Need to get home. Please help." The blue ink is faint, so you can barely see the words.

"It's better than nothing," he says.

Gio's wrong. In over an hour, we raise only $1.23. My Batman watch says that it's now 11:56, which would normally be bad luck because 1+1+5+6=13, but bad luck doesn't matter anymore. This is real. I have lice. My brain is in two pieces. My teeth are chattering. I hope I get arrested so that the Feds will blow cigarette smoke in my face to warm me up. At least they have beds in jail. I hope Phil doesn't bail me out.

A girl with red hair looks down but keeps walking. It isn't Ariel.

Fireflies are ugly in the city. They don't even light up. Flying black bugs—that's all they are. Even the pigeons are ugly here. And brave. They're not even scared of me. I just yelled "Rarrrrr" and it only scared Gio. The pigeons come even closer; their heads bounce back and forth like ping-pong balls. I wonder what they think about. Probably the same things I do: Will I last the night? What will I eat in the morning? If I don't sleep, will I die?

I wish I had my Batman cape.

I'm not really here. I'm home watching cartoons. I haven't seen Phil since he left us. And Ariel is still an Angel.

No, Ariel isn't even real. Never was. And neither was Phil.

And this, begging for money on the streets of New York City, definitely isn't real.

Except it is.

And so are they.

It's 12:05. Only nine minutes have passed since the last time I checked. The sun should rise in six hours.

"Hey, Gio," I say. "Do you want to hear a joke?"

"No," he says, so I tell myself: "Knock knock." "Who's there?" "Interrupting cow." "Interrupting cow wh—?" "Moooooooooooooooo!"

Don't get in the cab, Ariel. Please don't get in the cab, Ariel. The driver is reckless. No, he is drunk. You don't have enough money for a taxi anyway. Your sisters are evil Smartypants. Let's go back in the club. I want to dance. I'm a fast learner. I'm a late bloomer, but a fast learner. Let me show you.

The truth, Ariel, is this . . .

My face hurts. My cheeks are numb. I'm wearing two black T-shirts, two pairs of white socks, and my gray sweatshirt but I think I'm getting frostbite, which means they'll have to cut off my legs, arms, or ears. I would rather lose my arms than my legs, so that I could still walk around. No, I would rather lose my ears because that way I couldn't hear the nasty things that Ariel and Phil are saying about me.

If someone gives us more than a dollar, I promise to do homework. If three people in a row give money, I will give Phil a second chance even though he doesn't deserve it. If someone gives us twenty dollars, I will go home.

It's 1:00. Hickory, dickory, dock, the mouse ran up the clock . . .

Gio has a new strategy. When somebody walks by, he stands up and holds out his sign and begs for help. When nobody is walking by, he lies back down on the concrete and writes in his notebook. Like a poet. This is why Gio dragged me to New York City: so he could sleep in a gutter and write about it.

Did he use me? Are we really friends? I want to ask him but I need to conserve the only warm thing I have left: my breath. It's a leaky faucet; it seeps through my nose, through my mouth. I can only imagine how much heat I will lose if I speak.

If I argue, I could die instantly.

Maybe someone will bring me leftover pizza like I did to the blue-eyed guy with the gray blanket outside Joe's Pizza. Somewhere, Phil is laughing at me—again.

I feel an emergency coming, which at least breaks up my night. I am already that old guy who has nothing to look forward to except his next toilet break. But I don't have to go #2. I only have to go #1.

I distract myself so that I can hold it. I spy with my little eye something . . . red. The wrapper for Big Red gum. I spy with my little eye something . . . green. The gas station sign. I spy with my little eye something . . . blue. The label of that empty beer bottle. I spy with my little eye something . . . hot. I can't find anything hot, so I lose.

I switch games. My left hand loses to my right hand at thumb war. Best out of three. Best out of seven. Best out of nineteen.

I pee in the gutter and don't wash my hands.

Gio stands up and begs for more money. He remains standing for over an hour. I rip a piece of paper out of his notebook and grab the blue pen. I start writing. My eyes are throbbing, but I continue to write. It makes me lighter, but it doesn't make me any warmer.

Gio is sleeping.

Down the street, a man yells into a pay phone. "GOD DAMN IT! ANOTHER BILL? ALWAYS ANOTHER DAMN BILL!"

The man is the first person I've seen in hours.

He looks at the ground for something to kick but there's nothing around: no rocks, no soccer balls, no pigeons. The man covers his face with his hands. I can hear him grunting. He pulls at his hair on both sides.

He brings the phone to his ear. "I'm sorry for yelling, honey. I get off work in a few hours. I'll be home soon. You know how the buses are. All right. I love you. And tell Teresa I love her. Tuck her in for me. Okay, honey. Goodbye."

He walks toward me. I stand up and raise the cardboard sign as he approaches.

He's wearing a light blue jacket, a button-down white shirt, and black pants. His skin is pale and his eyes are red. There are heavy bags under his eyes, drooping like my grandpa's used to as his memory slipped out the back door and never returned.

"Just need to get home. Please help," I say, pointing to our sign in case he is blind.

"What are you doing?" he asks, sounding annoyed.

I don't answer him because he is a stranger, an extremely mad stranger, in a strange city at a strange time, which makes me feel like this is another scary scene in a scary movie.

"Are you a mute?" he grunts.

I look at my shoelaces. They used to be white; now they're the color of Cookies 'n Cream ice cream with a lot of cookies in it.

He takes a deep breath. "How old are you?"

"Fourteen," I tell him.

"You from around here?"

"No."

"How'd you get here?"

"Bus."

"You go to school?"

"Yes, but not today."

"But you *do* go to school . . ."

"Yes. I go to Radcliffe High School."

He smiles. "You made it to high school . . ."

"Yes."

"But you're gonna quit now?"

"I—"

He takes a deep breath and blows it in my face. It smells like morning.

"Do you know how many nights I lie awake at night wishing that I had graduated high school?"

I shake my head.

He raises his left eyebrow. "More than you've been alive."

"That's a lot."

"Son, why are you here?"

"Because of Phil."

"Your dad?"

"How'd you know?"

"Ain't it always about the father?"

"That's what Gio says."

"That guy right there?" he asks, pointing at a sleeping Gio.

I nod.

"Son, do you like school?"

"Some days."

"Can you read?"

I nod.

"Can you write?"

"Gio is teaching me," I tell him.

"You workin' on something there?" he says, pointing to my notebook.

"Kind of."

"Can I read it?"

Since it's easier to be naked in front of strangers, I show him my poem:

The Bus
by Rene

I'm shivering outside a restaurant
on 16th street running
late for the 1:35 to New York
did I forget to leave the tip
who knows I know I'm
late five minutes five
blocks it's still
possible if I run stop
thinking start running keep
going two more
blocks I think it's still there one
more block yes one
ticket one New
York ticket please still here
thank God thank
you man it's crowded there

are no seats left
thank God there's one in
the back excuse me excuse
me coming through and
she has hazel eyes
hello can I sit thank you hello
your name my name I'm
from you're from she has
hazel eyes and red
hair why won't she
talk to me say
something tell her
something maybe she'll
smile back and maybe
someday I'll have
dinner with her father one
on one for all the
glory and I'll say I don't
know sir what I want to
do with myself but I love
your daughter more than
anything in the
world and he'll look me in the
eye and say wake
up wake up it's
Tuesday wake
up it's 10 a.m. get
dressed

"That's . . . interesting," he says. "Clunky, but charming."

"Is that a good thing?"

"It's a freshman thing. Speaking of which, why ain't you at Heathcliffe High School?" he asks.

"You mean Radcliffe High School."

He looks annoyed. "Heathcliffe, Radcliffe, Mountcliffe, whatever! Look, you can probably tell by the uniform"—he opens his coat and points to a McDonald's nametag with the name "George" under the golden arches—"that I didn't get no high school diploma or my GED."

"What's a GED?" I ask.

"It's a second chance that's even harder than the first. You gotta enroll in courses 'cause you don't remember everything you learned in high school—even if you went to class, which most of us didn't. So the classes are full of knuckleheads. You know what I mean by knuckleheads?"

"Johnny Van Slyke," I tell him.

"Okay. Imagine having thirty Johnny Van Slykes in your room."

I do what he says and imagine it. It makes me want to throw up, which would not be doomsday because I haven't eaten anything except a few bites of raw fish, so there wouldn't be much to throw up.

"Besides the knuckleheads," he says, "there are fewer classes, the teachers are tired and pissed off that nobody comes . . . the pits, man, the pits."

"Oh."

"Yeah, *oh*," he says. "Look, I'd help you with money, but as you can see by the golden arches on my shirt, I ain't got a whole lotta dough."

"It's okay."

"Here," he says, handing me a handful of coins. "If you spend it on anything other than a ride home, I will come back here and chop off your legs. Understand?"

IT'S 2:19 A.M. ONLY FOUR MORE HOURS OF DARKNESS. GIO IS sleeping. His right hand is wrapped around our Styrofoam money cup. I reach in and count the coins: $2.17. Because we need better luck, I spill the coins onto the pavement and pick up only the ones that are heads up.

Now we have ninety-three cents.

I wish the sun would rise. If only I could hear a rooster. Someday, if I ever make it back home, I'll get a rooster to wake me up instead of an alarm clock. I'll name him "Gio." He'll be funny and different and dangerous.

But I'm allergic to roosters.

THE COLD AIR BITES MY SKIN LIKE A SHARP COMEBACK. IT chomps away, tearing into my flesh until I can no longer feel it.

My hands are numb. I pick up a safety pin from the ground and stick it into my thumb. I feel no pain. I feel a crashing wave of terror, though, because I just stuck a dirty safety pin that could have been contaminated with AIDS or cancer or lice or sperm into my thumb! What's wrong with me? I must be losing brain cells. Maybe I really *do* have brain damage.

I look at my reflection in a broken Budweiser bottle. My ears are the color of blood; I wish they were as warm. If I cut myself with the Budweiser bottle, prick my index finger, will I warm up?

The answer to that question is "No."

THE COLD IS MY ENEMY.

It is my antagonist. The Tybalt to my Mercutio. The Joker to my Batman. The Lex Luther to my Superman.

The cold is my kryptonite. It saps my superpowers. I am Clark Kent, dying a slow human death on a sidewalk. But there are no movie cameras, not even a surveillance camera to capture this moment. There is no heroic comeback, and no Lois Lane. She took the first taxi out of town.

No, wait, it's my movie. I'll write my own ending. She returned! Ariel and I made it out of town. We hitchhiked with a band of hippies all the way out West; now we're wearing cowboy hats, dancing a jig on the beach. The sand is hot enough to fry our toenails. That's why we're dancing.

"Ariel," I say. "Stop dancing for a second. I have a surprise."

I reach into my pocket to pull out the ring. I can't feel the ring. My hands are numb. I dig in further and pull my arm out. My hand is still in my pocket.

"Don't worry, Rene," she says. "It's just frostbite."

"But my hand!"

"Don't be frightened. *Frostbite* isn't even a scary word. It sounds almost the same as *Frosty.* So you *almost* accomplished your mission."

She laughs.

"YO, BROTHER MAN, IS IT MORNING YET?" GIO ASKS.

I glance at my watch. Three hours and eighteen minutes more.

"I'm sorry," he says. "For everything."

Gio looks human—too human. My fallen hero, there is no sparkle in your eyes, only a dim light. So this is where a free spirit comes to die: on a cold slab of concrete.

"Can you feel your hands?" he asks.

I wonder where my mom is right now. She never sent out a search party. Maybe she never will. Maybe she chose Phil over me.

"What are we gonna do?" he asks.

Fifty meters away is a pay phone, the one where George from McDonald's made a phone call. I *could* call my mom, but I'm afraid of what she has to say about Phil. This is the ultimate scary scene in a scary movie. No, this isn't a movie! It's real life! It's *my* life. And my mom was the one who always told me to assert myself if I don't understand. I don't understand something right now. And there's only one way to find out.

"I'm calling my mom," I declare.

Gio looks wounded. For the record, I'm sorry I ever compared myself to Clark Kent. I only said that to warm myself up. Gio's the real Clark Kent. Conceding defeat is a slap in

Clark's face; calling parents is a roundhouse punch in the chops. He's bleeding from his mouth. I'm sure of it. The metallic taste humbles him. I can see it in his eyes.

"Brother man," he says softly. Clark Kent may sound like he's dying, but he never dies in the movies. He always rallies. He summons up his strength and fights like a warrior, like the superhero he is (or was) in the final battle.

"Give me a chance," he pleads. "Give me the morning. I will pluck us out of this pickle jam."

This is his final battle. I will allow him to fight.

He closes his eyes, so I do, too.

JOHNNY VAN SLYKE HAS RETURNED. WE'RE BACK IN SCHOOL, back in the bathroom. Norman the hyena is with us, too.

"What do you say we give him a swirley?" Johnny says.

Norman falls onto the filthy floor in a fit of laughter.

"What's a swirley?" I ask, because that's what my mom would want me to do.

"You don't know?" Norman's eyes light up. "You really *don't know?"*

I shake my head, hoping lice will fall out and blind Norman and Johnny in all four of their eyeballs.

"He really *doesn't know!" Norman shouts. "He* really *doesn't know!"*

The lice don't seem to be falling out, so I shake my head harder, faster.

"It's when we put your head in the toilet and flush," Johnny says, drunk with excitement.

"We basically flush you down the toilet," Norman explains, then falls down again.

I must escape. But the exit is blocked off by Phil, who stands with his arms folded like a bouncer.

I call for Gio to help but he is asleep on the bathroom floor. "The floor is dirty and cold!" I yell. "Wake up!" He doesn't hear me because my voice has disappeared. No sound escapes, only air, visible to my trained eyes because it's freezing cold in the bathroom.

A mug full of hot chocolate sits on top of the faucet. That would warm me up. But it could also make me puke. Puke is warm, though. It would warm me up on the way down and *the way out. I reach for it. Phil slaps at my hand and pours the drink down the drain.*

"That'll give you something to write about," Phil says.

Johnny and Norman shove me into a stall.

Then I hear a sound, a beautiful sound: the sound of a new day. It's so loud that it must be coming from inside of the bathroom. I drop to the dirty floor and peek into the next stall.

Red and orange feathers, black eyes, and a yellow beak. A rooster is singing.

I sneeze.

"I'VE GOT IT, BROTHER MAN," GIO SAYS, SHAKING ME.

There's a light around his face. He looks like Jesus H. Christ.

"Wake up," he says. "We made it."

That's when I realize it's morning. Batman says it's 6:16,

which is a bad luck time because 6+1+6=13, but since I've been waiting for the sun for years and years and years, I don't close my eyes and wait another minute; I stand up and listen to his plan.

He waves his arms excitedly. "You know how we're reading *Romeo and Juliet* in Mr. Head's class?"

"We didn't read the play; we watched the movie."

"Same story. Listen to me: like us, both Romeo and Juliet were in a pickle jam, right?"

I nod.

"An even bigger pickle jam than we're in right now, right?"

I nod.

"They were desperate, really desperate, so they decided it was okay to trick people."

I nod.

"So they pretended to be sick. No, dead. They pretended to be something they weren't, right?"

I nod.

"Brother man, you're going to play sick. No, dead. I don't know, one of those two. And people are going to give us money. It's our ticket home."

I believe in his plan until he says, "Everything will be fine. You'll see."

"PLEASE HELP! FOR THE LOVE OF GOD, SOMEBODY PLEASE HELP!"

Gio is holding me in his arms and screaming as if he and I are the lone survivors in a scary scene in a scary movie.

Last time I checked I was ninety-seven pounds. Given my age, the rapid development of my body, and last night's sushi dinner, I've probably ballooned to ninety-eight pounds. That's why Gio's arms are starting to shake. I'm about to fall. Maybe that's his plan. We haven't talked about that part. All he said for me to do was to close my eyes and not move a muscle.

"HELP! SOMEBODY PLEASE HELP! GOD, WHERE ARE YOU? WILL SOMEBODY PLEASE HELP!"

I'm not allowed to peek at my Batman watch because that would require opening my eyes and moving a muscle, maybe even two or three muscles.

But I've been counting: 189 seconds have passed since he picked me up. I don't think he'll make it to 200 seconds because his arms are shaking and any second he will drop me. It starts to rain.

I'm slipping through Gio's fingers.

200 seconds, 201, 202, 203.

"A *QUARTER*? THIS KID IS DYING!"

Surely Gio will drop me; he is Clark Kent, a human being . . . 207 seconds. It's raining harder.

"A *DOLLAR*? A KID IS DYING SO YOU GIVE HIM A *DOLLAR*! WE GOTTA GET HIM ON A BUS!"

Gio's plan isn't going to work. Even *I* know that dying people don't get thrown on buses. They get thrown on—

Sirens ring in the distance. Sirens ring around the corner. Sirens ring across the street. I can see the flashing red and blue lights even with my eyes closed. Screeching tires. More wheels; these are louder, closer. A firm, male voice approaches.

"Sir, we received a call. Load him onto the stretcher. We need to get him to a hospital."

Gio grips me tighter and shouts, "NO! WE DON'T HAVE INSURANCE! WE NEED TO GET THIS BOY *HOME*!"

"This boy needs immediate medical assistance. That's why we're here. Hand him over!"

Strong hands are wrestling with Gio's. I am caught in the crossfire of desperate fingers. 218 seconds. I'm slipping. 219 seconds. Gio whirls me around. And then his arms give out. 220 seconds. I come crashing down on concrete.

"RUN!" Gio yells.

He tugs at my right arm until I stand up and start running then sprinting through buckets and buckets of rain, and even though I hear sirens following me then gaining on me, I don't look back until Gio tells me it's safe to stop.

MY CLOTHES—AND I'M WEARING ALL OF THEM—ARE A filthy heap of sweat and rain. If I could hang myself on a clothesline to dry for an afternoon, I would.

But it's still raining. We take cover under the awning of a bagel store with a large sign for "appetizing smoked fish," which reminds me of Mr. Head, who taught me about oxymorons, like "jumbo shrimp" or "open secret," as in Gio's desire to continue is an open secret because he gets down on the ground and begs, "Please, Rene, for me, please. Give me one more chance to make this right."

A dying man's final plea. What choice do I have? We don't have enough money for a bus. Even if we did, there's no way

Ron the bus driver would let me on with wet clothes. I mean, Ron's a nice guy—he did say "You're welcome" when I thanked him for safely driving me to the city—but he didn't strike me as a man I could push over.

"What do you have in mind?" I ask.

"Just wait here," he says. "I promise. It'll only be a minute." He waves goodbye, then dashes into the pouring rain. I wave back.

And then I am alone. Again. I want to smell my left hand over and over again, but there's something funny in my head. I don't know what it is or why it's funny but I can't stop laughing. Louder and louder and louder until my cheeks are sore and I've given myself the hiccups. I hear someone approaching, but it doesn't stop me from laughing.

I open my eyes. Gio is holding two small black umbrellas. Except for his tall hair, he is a dead-on ringer for Clark Kent. His left eye is red. The right side of his face is swollen. Blood trickles from his left nostril.

"Okay, Rene," he says, "let's call your mom."

"Oh, thank God! Thank God you're okay."

I can tell she's crying because her voice is shaking like a tambourine.

I want her to stop talking, not because I don't like hearing her voice but because I need to listen for crashing movement, snide comments, grunts, grumbles.

There's no background noise yet, but any second Phil will scream into the phone that I am a dirty, stupid moron.

"Honey, are you alone?" she asks. I want to ask her the same thing, but not knowing is better than her saying "No, I'm not alone," so I answer her question: "Gio is here, too. We are safe."

"Where is *here*, honey?"

"New York City."

"Oh, God! Are you safe?"

"I just said we were."

"Are you hungry?"

"No," I lie.

"Thirsty?"

I lie again.

"Cold?"

Another lie.

I want to stop lying and ask the important question, but I remind myself again that not knowing is better than hearing bad news. For years, Phil was the 800-pound gorilla in the room I didn't want to acknowledge and my mom didn't want to forget. Even over the phone, Phil is a gorilla.

"Oh, thank God you're okay. I haven't slept a wink . . ."

Good.

"I've been worrying and worrying . . ."

Good.

"I'm so angry with myself . . ."

Good.

"Rene, there's so much I wanted to tell you, needed to tell you, *should* have told you, but the moment was never right and then you ran off . . . But I don't blame you . . . Rene, you were right about your father—"

"You mean Phil."

"Yes, Phil, you can call him whatever you like, Rene. He needs help. You were right about that and . . ."

Here it comes: he may need help but he's her husband for better or for worse; the man without whom I wouldn't exist; the only father I have, who may have flaws but who gave me shelter and new clothes and envelopes in the mail and money and sometimes love—

"He needs help, and, Rene, I tried to help him. Maybe I shouldn't have, but he sounded terrible, almost suicidal, and he was in trouble, big trouble. His gambling got worse and he was using again. Rene, he has an addictive personality and I—"

"He has a terrible personality."

"Well, yes, Rene, he does, but he was in over his head and he contacted me and said he was in town, and I shouldn't have but I tried to help get him back on his feet, and I spent a lot of time at night trying to help him and—"

"That's why you weren't home when I slept at the school?"

"Yes, honey, and I'm so sorry, I really am, but I didn't want him coming over to the house and upsetting you so I met him somewhere else, but then you didn't come back that night and I knew I couldn't keep it up any longer, and he begged to see you, and I felt like I didn't have a choice. I know now that I did, Rene, I *did* have a choice, but I felt like I was drowning. I'm so sorry, Rene, I really am, but I still made Phil keep his distance—I made him sleep in the car instead of in the house; he never slept in the house, Rene, even when he was making pancakes, he spent the night before in his car—and I didn't want you to see him without me, but you were in trouble at school and someone needed to come get you and I couldn't get out of work or else I would've been fired, and then you didn't let me explain . . . But it was my fault and I don't blame you, I don't . . ."

She is crying into the phone. I listen closely to each one of her sobs to see if Phil is anywhere near her.

"Rene, if anything were to happen to you . . . I wouldn't . . ." Her nose is running; she sniffles the snot back up her nose. There are no other noises in the background. "I'd be so lost,

Rene, if you . . ." More sniffles, more snot. "I can't lose you . . . I can't . . . I can't . . . I . . ." She is crying so much and so loud that I can't hear the voices inside my head. All I hear is her crying. I can't even hear Phil . . . unless he's whispering like a rattlesnake.

"But when I saw what Phil had done to you, Rene, at dinner, and I saw how angry and upset you got when he was around, I knew I couldn't help Phil anymore, because I couldn't bear the thought of losing you. Phil's not here anymore, Rene. He needs to figure it out for himself . . . You helped me realize that, and I thank you for that and I love you. I love you so, so much."

I want her to say it, say the word, *the* word, but she's not the type. She's not going to say it, not tonight or tomorrow or the next day. But she doesn't have to say it; I know it to be true.

I am a superhero.

THAT WAS SEVENTY-SEVEN DAYS AGO.

At school, people tell me I look different.

Those people are liars. I might have grown half an inch in my sleep, but that happens to everyone, except old people like Milton and Edith.

Radcliffe High School definitely hasn't changed. I don't think it ever will. I still go to class, Mr. Chalmers still sniffles, the Bigbulletholes still shoot themselves in the ear, and gym unfortunately still exists.

Christmas vacation is a week away, and Mr. Head hasn't quit yet, which is a good sign he'll come back for second semester and hopefully last the rest of the year. He doesn't need anyone to save him anymore, that's for sure. Just the other day, I heard Norman the hyena say, "Damn, I feel like I can't even *breathe* in Mr. Head's room."

Every now and then, though, when Mr. Head has puddles under his arms or sighs after a really long class or walks down the hallway with his head down, I put my hand on his shoulder and tell him that even superheroes have bad days.

Instead of groaning like a dying old man, or hanging his

head like a limp animal, he laughs, and then asks me if I'm enjoying the comic books he gave me. "In which issue does Batman have his worst day ever?" . . . "How did he turn it around?" . . . "Which superhero sweats as much as I do?" . . . "Which superheroes aren't afraid to ask for help?" He says he doesn't want me to tell him the answers; he wants me to write them—and any *other* thoughts—in a journal.

I bring that journal with me to Ms. Adelman. Yeah, I'm talking to her more now, even though her office still gives me nightmares. It's weird, but she wants me to tell her about those nightmares. So, this morning I said, "I dreamt that the pills the other doctor gave me suddenly stopped working, and I couldn't do my homework because I was playing ping-pong for twenty straight hours while lying naked and homeless outside a dance club."

She said it's "perfectly normal," but I'm not so sure. All I know is that I don't *need* to be perfectly normal. I don't even *want* to be perfect. *Or* normal. I just want to be able to walk and talk and sleep in my own skin, as long as it's warm. Recently, it has been.

Especially at home. Sometimes my mom and I tell each other jokes during dinner: There are two blueberry muffins baking in the oven. One muffin says to the other, "Damn, it's hot in here." The other muffin says, "Oh my God, a talking muffin!" . . . A pirate walks into a bar with a steering wheel bulging out of his pants. The bartender says, "Hey pirate, what's with the steering wheel?" The pirate looks down at his pants and says, "Arrrr, it's driving me nuts." Here's another one—it's tough to write, but it's my second favorite joke: What do you call a fish with no eyes? "Fsh." (The fish has no *i*'s. Get it?)

Johnny Van Slyke doesn't bother me anymore. Apparently, he bit the wrong student in the shoulder, because Johnny got beaten up so badly by an upperclassman that he transferred to another school so that it wouldn't happen again. The important thing to remember is that he never would've been transferred had he not been suspended in the first place. Do you remember why he was suspended in the first place? Me. That's right. Me.

Ariel is still an Angel. Sometimes, during lunch, she walks over to Gio and me at our table and gives us some of her food. Anything she brings over is delicious, but I like it best when she brings over sushi, because it's an inside joke that I am on the inside of.

Usually, she sits down for a few minutes and talks to us about bus rides and museums and cities. She says we should do it again—after we graduate in three years. She talks to me almost as much as she talks to Gio, so I know that I don't have anything to worry about. Besides, Ariel told us both that she's far too busy for a boyfriend.

Gio, like my mom, thinks I am a superhero because I saved him and Mr. Head, but he doesn't say it. It's not something guys talk about. But we do talk a lot about what happened that night and why it went down the way it did. He believes it was his destiny, his mission, to fail in the city. He still wants to be a poet, but not as much as he used to. One night in the gutter was enough for him. Now he just wants to pass his classes. He asked me how to do it. I'm no expert or anything, but I know that going to class is important. Gio goes to his classes. All of them. Well, most of them. Okay, about half of them.

Gio doesn't do a whole lot of homework, so sometimes I help him with it; other times Mr. Head does. This week, it was Mr. Head's turn to help Gio with homework. I met up with Gio after. On Friday afternoon, he laughed the whole way home, retelling a story Mr. Head had just told him.

"Check it out, brother man," Gio began. "On the way to school this morning, this kid found a bat flapping its broken wing on the ground. I know what you're thinking, 'What's a bat doing on the ground in broad daylight?' Maybe he got hurt the night before. Who knows? Anyway, this kid feels bad for the bat. He doesn't want to just leave him there to die. I mean, how often do you see a bat dying on your way to school? So, there's a Dumpster not too far from him and he digs through the garbage until he finds a small box and a stick. He nudges the bat into the box with the stick.

"Then he takes it to school, where he runs the box up to Mr. Head's room and asks for his advice. Can you imagine Mr. Head looking at a dying bat? Crazy, right? So, Mr. Head suggests calling the Department of Environmental Conservation. He does. The kid is relieved until he gets nervous that they're going to kill the bat. 'They'll put him to sleep!' he cries. 'They'll kill him!' You should have heard Mr. Head describing this. Anyway, the kid runs out of the room and down the stairs toward the nurse's office. Mr. Head chugs after him. Can you imagine? Somehow, the kid gets past the receptionist until the nurse screams. Like, a bloodcurdling scream."

"You mean like in a scary scene in a scary movie?" I asked.

"Exactly," he said. "The nurse screams *so* loud that Mr. Head said his ears popped. And Mr. Head's got some big ears. Anyway, the receptionist runs to the examining room and yells, 'GET THAT DIRTY BAT OUT OF HERE. NOW!' The kid dashes out of the room and smacks into Mr. Head, who offers to talk about it over lunch."

That was just one story. There have been others. Hopefully, there will be many more. Gio and I walk home together every day, unless I'm staying after school for writers' club.

I want to write a book. Maybe about the kid with his bat. I mean, a month or two ago, it could have been me saving a bat—or a pigeon—and hiding it in my locker, feeding it between classes until it died and rotted and stank up the whole school until everyone found out and called me "dead-bat kid," or "bat freak," or, if I was lucky, "Batman."

Actually, I already started writing a book. It's about things I love, things I hate, things I want to do, things I've already done, things I want to be, things I almost am . . .

And things that make me b'noodles.

Acknowledgments

I would like to thank my editor, Janine O'Malley, and everyone else at FSG for making every step of the writing process a creative and joyful exchange of ideas.

My agent, Michelle Andelman, is a smart and supportive writing partner. I am grateful to have her on my side.

My wife and her family's kindness and grace made a busy year of teaching, wedding planning, and book writing not only feasible but fun.

My mom, Amy, as well as cousins Marlene Newman and Deb Salkind, reviewed early drafts and gave helpful feedback. I am thankful for their love and their love of writing.

The enthusiasm from my dad, Andy, and brother, Jared, meant the world to me.

A special shout-out to my ninth- and tenth-grade English students, especially those who read sections of the first draft and told me it was "O.D. good" and "mad funny." And to "keep on rockin' with your awesome writing." I can only hope I've encouraged them as much as they have me.

COUNTY LIBRARY
TILLAMOOK, ORE.
DISCARD